INTO A STAR

INTO A STAR

Puk Qvortrup

Translated by Hazel Evans

HAMISH HAMILTON
an imprint of
PENGUIN BOOKS

HAMISH HAMILTON

UK | USA | Canada | Ireland | Australia
India | New Zealand | South Africa

Hamish Hamilton is part of the Penguin Random House group of companies
whose addresses can be found at global.penguinrandomhouse.com.

First published in Danish as *Indien stjerne* by GRIF, 2019
First published in this translation by Hamish Hamilton, 2024
001

This book is published with the support of The Society of Authors and the Authors' Foundation

Danish Arts
Foundation

This book is published with the support of the Danish Arts Foundation

Lyrics on p. 154 from 'You've Got the Love' by The Source

Extract from Edward Broadbridge's translation of 'Nu falmer skoven trindt om land' by N. F. S. Grundtvig,
English language copyright © 2008 Edward Broadbridge, reproduced by permission of Edward Broadbridge

Extract from Hazel Evans's translation of 'Ind i en Stjerne' by Morten Nielsen,
English language copyright © 2024 Hazel Evans, reproduced by permission of Hazel Evans

Set in 12.75/15.5 pt Fournier MT Std
Typeset by Jouve (UK), Milton Keynes
Printed and bound in Great Britain by Clays Ltd, Elcograf S.p.A.

The authorized representative in the EEA is Penguin Random House Ireland,
Morrison Chambers, 32 Nassau Street, Dublin D02 YH68

A CIP catalogue record for this book is available from the British Library

ISBN: 978–0–241–68222–7

www.greenpenguin.co.uk

MIX
Paper | Supporting
responsible forestry
FSC® C018179

Penguin Random House is committed to a
sustainable future for our business, our readers
and our planet. This book is made from Forest
Stewardship Council® certified paper.

To our children

Night gathers all things near.

A deafening
silence in vastness.

——We walk together, hand in hand
into a star.

Morten Nielsen, 1943

Three in the bed. One not yet born, another dead, and I'm alive.

Someone has placed a sheet over us, electric candles around us. Two men are standing at the foot of the bed, crying. Brother, they say, the word foreign on their lips. Two parents are sitting hunched over beside us, turned grey by the night's events. She says something, cries. Then they're gone.

I lie on my side, facing him. The sheet billows about my hip and comes to rest motionless over the contours of his body. It doesn't look right, he never lies on his back. He's been put like that, got ready. For me, for this.

A bluish-white forehead, arms limp. Naked apart from a pair of baggy hospital trousers. It can't have been easy to get him into them.

The plastic mattress protests as I attempt our usual embrace: one leg flung around him, one arm. But he's too heavy, I can't pull him into me, my stomach is in the way.

Under the sheet it smells of resignation and faeces, soap and rubbing alcohol.

A swollen face that still bears the trace of the oxygen mask around his mouth. The rust-coloured freckles on his shoulder even more pronounced against the now-waxlike skin. I can just about make out a dark mass of dried blood in one nostril – the last of the reddest of reds that used to flow from every hole, every pinprick.

I close my eyes and whisper that it's OK, we can just pretend we're at home in bed. Soon our son will wake up in his cot, and hey, listen, the gulls are squawking outside again – remember last summer when a man came out on to his balcony one morning and shouted at them to fuck off? And we lay laughing in our double bed, our eyes still shut?

My words turn to drivel on his skin. I fall silent, wishing I could fall into eternal sleep with him instead, but the chill of his body won't let me.

The baby is awake again now, rolling around inside me, playfully pushing and kicking at his dad's body, his liveliness untimely.

I caress the little triangle of chest hair like I always do, but it doesn't feel the same. The cold drives me out from under the sheet, and the baby and I roll over and slide from the bed. My feet make contact with the floor; my socks are all bunched up.

I take one last look – at the round suction marks left by the heart monitor on his chest, like crop circles after UFO landings; at his lips, slightly parted – and I lean in for a kiss. A kiss that belongs only to me. I no longer know this body; he isn't here.

He isn't here.

I

Our street lay in shade. I was almost home, but I couldn't get into the building. Locked out. On an otherwise beautiful September morning.

Everything from this point on would be *otherwise*.

The trees had begun to let go of the year. Deep reds, yellows and crispy browns littering the ground. The ghost of a sun hung softly in the sky; the air tasted of salt. A gust of wind swept the leaves up with a rasping sound as they bustled along the asphalt. Cars crawled by, bikes sped. It was that time of day, business as usual, the world moving on without me. I sat down on the stone steps by the front door and the cold began to creep through the thin material of my leggings.

My mum, my parents-in-law and my friend Helene threw little desperate questions to each other over my head.

Maybe his keys were with his shoes and clothes in the bag at the hospital? Do you think we could ring one of the neighbours' bells and ask them to let us in? Who'll do it?

My dad had taken my keys with him when he went to drop Elmer off at nursery – this wasn't something a two-year-old should be around to witness.

Helene had appeared out of nowhere at the hospital. She'd

linked her arm through mine and marched me through the corridors; I let myself be led. Now she was trying to wrap me in her puffer jacket and I protested. It was all the same to me, hot or cold.

Hans and Helle had just lost a son, but they kept asking me if I wasn't freezing.

I didn't want them. Didn't want them speaking to me, touching me. They reminded me of my continued existence and all I wanted was to disappear.

I sank my face into my hands, my cheekbones into my palms, my fingers into my eye sockets. The salt stuck my fringe to my forehead. I spread my fingers to let the tears out and the pavement shot up towards me. My elbows dug into my thighs to keep me from falling further, my pregnant belly making it impossible for me to sit up properly.

I threw back my head. A whimper escaped me, then made its way back down my throat and turned into a deep, guttural moan. *Åhh! Åhh! Åhh-åhh-åhh!*

I said his name between each *åhh*.

Our upstairs neighbour cycled past, his daughter in the child seat behind him. What's going on here? said his face. How ridiculous we must have looked: me sitting on the front steps, collapsed over my stomach, a semicircle of people gathered around me. I didn't care.

I was five metres above the earth, watching it all happen from a helium balloon. Reality was somewhere down there, I could hear myself crying, and on some level I must have known that my husband was dead – I'd just visited his corpse at the hospital, after all – but the knowledge had yet to sink in.

I figured there was still time to alter fate's course. I just had to pull myself together, come up with a solid counter-argument.

My mum's voice came from some distant underwater place. We must have got into the apartment because she was perched on the edge of our beige IKEA sofa. I lay under a duvet next to her.

She said to someone that I'd fallen asleep. She said I'd been watching videos of my husband on my phone. She said I should get something to eat.

Puggimus, she said, my little Puggimus.

The sofa cushion was soaked in saliva and tears, strands of my hair stuck to the coarse surface. I must have slept after all. I sat up, determined to make my own lunch, but my dad placated me with some of the birthday cake I'd baked the day before. I took a bite. The icing merged with the slime in my mouth and the cake expanded. I struggled to swallow.

A police officer called, and apologized for calling, but wanted to know if there was any chance my husband had taken euphoriant substances.

I asked if he meant EPO? Like Bjarne Riis, to improve his performance, was that what he meant?

It was.

He also wanted to know if I'd give them permission to conduct an autopsy. I gave them permission, and added that my husband wished to donate his organs, but they probably shouldn't bother with his corneas. He had such bad eyesight.

My voice sounded calm, and I felt momentarily proud of myself for keeping my wits about me.

The police officer cleared his throat. Unfortunately, due to my husband's condition, he wasn't eligible for organ donation.

Less than twenty-four hours ago, he'd assembled the little balance bike we gave Elmer for his birthday. Now he was about to be pulled apart, himself.

I retreated into my duvet hole. The air inside was humid and my breath brought out the smell of detergent from the linen. My parents had turned the TV on, but turned it off again when my phone rang for the second time.

This time it was a crisis counsellor. The system worked, leaped into action exactly as it was supposed to.

He asked if 5 p.m. was good for me. As if plans were something I might still have.

Out in the hall, my little sister Andrea and her new boyfriend stood clinging to each other. I made my way past them to get to the shoes. They jumped apart, eyeing me self-consciously. I eyed them back.

You're going to get married and you're going to have children together, I proclaimed, twisting my wedding ring around my finger.

They nodded and I turned to face my dad.

He was standing in the doorway, fidgeting with the car keys. We were going to be late.

I shared the same proclamation with the grief counsellor – a man I immediately assumed was gay. It crossed my mind that it was odd for me to be assuming anything about anyone at that moment, but then the thought was gone, archived.

We sat opposite each other in a pair of olive-green armchairs in a room that smelled of paint and was otherwise furnished with a coffee table, a pre-opened box of Kleenex, an empty desk and two identical desk lamps. A zipped-up computer bag rested against one of the walls.

It's important to get married, I said, and the counsellor nodded slowly. He brought his hands together, shook them lightly and looked up as if to thank the heavens, a ring glinting on his own left hand.

And to have children, I added.

He made a little half-grimace and his hands fell back down into his lap. This time I hadn't quite hit the mark.

I wiped my nose and rubbed my eyes. They were sore, but kept on running.

The tissue in my hand was now so wet I could sculpt it into a little bowl. I smoothed it between my fingers and did my best to make it perfect. I pressed the base of the bowl into the hollow of my palm and when a layer came loose, I fixed it back into place with more tears and snot. My fingertips were shrivelled like after a long bath.

The counsellor watched, said nothing.

I wondered what the bowl might say about me, what it might tell him that I didn't already know.

What I don't understand is why I don't feel more, I said in a strained voice.

That's because you're still in shock, he said, you have all the symptoms. Notice how you're breathing, you're hyper-ventilating.

Only now did I become aware of my ribcage. Convulsing in short, frantic jolts.

Tell me what happened, he said.

What had happened, I didn't really know. I'd received a call and then I was at Skejby Hospital and there was my husband, and at first he seemed to be alive but then he wasn't alive after all and they gave me some brochures to take home with unlit candles on the cover.

So now he's dead, the counsellor said, holding my gaze.

Yes? I whispered.

He repeated it.

Your husband is dead.

His goal was simple: to move me beyond the shock. This much I knew, but I was incapable of playing along and equally incapable of putting up a fight. We were conducting an emergency operation without anaesthetic. The counsellor's scalpel: my husband's name.

Lasse.

Lasse is dead, he said.

I heard the balloon above me pop. Everything burst into unbearable clarity.

I collapsed into myself.

Lasse was dead.

Never before had *forever* felt like such a physical sensation. It crushed me. Lasse was gone forever. He was just as gone this second as he was the previous one, as he would be for all the seconds to come. Whenever I'd thought about the future, Lasse had always been in it. Everything was suddenly possible, everything no longer existed.

Have you said anything to your son? the counsellor asked.

I shook my head, unable to speak. Elmer's dad was dead. The baby's dad was dead.

I'd left Elmer at home in the apartment with my mum and sisters and strictly forbidden them to say anything to him.

I couldn't even remember how he'd got home from nursery. Someone must have carried him up the stairs, helped him out of his raincoat and untied his laces. Probably when I'd been sitting slumped over in the shower with the water running over my neck and into my face. I didn't know how to talk to a two-year-old about death.

We only had fifteen minutes left of the appointment. I didn't want to go home, didn't want to stay here.

I couldn't remember the name of the man sitting opposite me, but he was the person who was to help me come up with the most important story of my life. A story I'd also have to tell my own child.

And there was no time to waste, said the counsellor. Elmer would already have sensed that something was amiss. But a two-year-old can't get his head around death, he said, it's too abstract. What he can understand is that Dad isn't coming home again, and then he needs to know where Dad is now.

So, heaven? Can we put him on a cloud? Bury him in the earth, burn him in a large oven? Do we believe in God? And why couldn't he have waited until tomorrow to die, so I'd have time to pull myself together first?

But heaven is big, clouds drift away, the earth is cold, ovens are for pizzas, God is Nobody, time is running out and Dad has run away.

II

Lasse's death smelled of cardamom. The death itself smelled of many things, but my first memory of it was of cardamom and soft butter buns.

It was Sunday morning. I'd baked a kagemand for the first time in my life and managed to pull it off. We were celebrating two days in advance – Sunday was better than Tuesday, then we'd have the whole afternoon, and the birthday boy was too young to know the difference anyway. Our guests were still somewhere on the motorway between Vojens and Aarhus. Lasse was still running his half-marathon, and running late as usual, but today I was determined not to let it bother me. Everything was ready.

Birthday bunting hung from the living-room ceiling; the balloons we'd rubbed on our clothes to make them static now stuck to the walls.

I'd find the same balloons piled in the cot when I got back from the intensive-care unit, Elmer's duvet draped over them like a flying carpet. But for now, the cot held only Elmer, taking a nap.

His new bike stood up against the living-room wall. It was quiet.

In the kitchen I inhaled the sweet, spiced smell of cake and shifted my weight from one foot to the other. The icing was still a bit runny but just about stiffening up. I broke its crispy surface as I decorated it with sweets. Liquorice for the eyes, toffee laces for the hair. I was about to do the nose and mouth when the phone rang.

An unknown number.

A doctor from Skejby Hospital. He wanted to know, was I Lasse's wife?

I couldn't help the wave of irritation that swept over me. He'd be sitting in A&E with a twisted ankle, he ought to have built up more slowly before attempting a half-marathon, it was so typical of him to push himself like this, an accident waiting to happen.

I'm afraid it's serious, the doctor said.

What do you mean? I asked in a voice that didn't sound like my own.

He tried to speak calmly. Said something about cardiac arrest, and that Lasse's heart wasn't beating by itself yet. That he'd been getting cardiac massage from a machine. He told me the name of the machine.

What the fuck was he talking about?

No, I interrupted. Tentative at first, then shouting. Over and over I shouted, screamed, at him. What was he trying to tell me?

He told me to come to the cardiac unit. The name of an entrance, then a number, a letter.

I can't figure all that out, I cried, you'll have to send an ambulance!

I was still shouting when I heard Elmer crying from his cot. See, now my son has woken up!

And it was as if a switch inside me flipped. All of a sudden, I was calm. A sharply focused, remote kind of calm. I felt the blood draining from my pounding head, the sweat on my hands turn to ice.

I cleared my throat and said I was ready now; I'd pulled myself together.

Elmer was still crying, but it would have to wait. I found a pad of paper and a pen, clicked the pen out, wrote down the doctor's name and phone number, and confirmed we'd meet at the entrance to the cardiac unit. The number. The letter. I asked if I could bring Elmer with me, but that wasn't such a good idea.

Before hanging up, I added:

Just so you know, I'm six months pregnant. Please try to remember that, in case I'm not able to.

I sat facing the doctor in a room at Skejby Hospital. A nurse had decided that she and I should hold hands.

The doctor spoke slowly, without breaking eye contact. Whenever he frowned, I mirrored him, nodding along as if I understood what was being said. I was waiting to hear that Lasse would be all right, but as soon as the doctor said he couldn't say for sure, nothing else went in.

Lasse's heart hadn't started beating by itself yet, he was in a coma and had been cooled down to prevent brain damage – but I couldn't figure out what any of this information had to do with anything.

When would I be able to see him?

Soon.

Was there anyone I wanted them to call for me?

His mum and dad.

Wouldn't I prefer to call them myself?

I didn't think I was up to it.

Roughly when did they think I'd be able to see him?

Soon enough, as soon as he'd stabilized.

Was there anyone who could come and keep me company?

My parents and two of my siblings were on their way.

Were we talking ten minutes or two hours until I'd be able to see him?

It was hard to say, they were doing everything they could.

The nurse stayed with me until my parents arrived. I didn't know if I was supposed to talk to her, but I didn't want to be rude. She led me over to an armchair with a footstool and I let myself sink down into it. She brought me a glass of squash, but my hands were shaking so much I nearly spilled it all over myself.

I placed one hand on my stomach. The baby always seemed to wake up whenever I sat or lay down, and did so now, kicking himself unapologetically around.

The door opened. I hoped it was the doctor returning with good news, but it was my parents, brother and sister, their faces askew. They bent over the chair to hug me.

My dad spoke to the nurse in hushed tones and my mum pulled up a chair next to mine. Emma and Asbjørn sat with their heads bowed, little droplets of water hitting the floor below them.

It felt wrong to be sitting with my feet up like I was in a spa. I must have said as much, because a bed was wheeled in for me.

I asked for the shoulder bag I'd hung over a chair earlier. Inside was my phone and the lunch Lasse had prepared for Elmer that morning. Rye bread and pâté.

There was a message from my friend Pernille, a photo of Elmer sitting in a sandpit digging with a plastic spade. He was doing fine, she wrote, and could stay with them as long as needed.

I'd thrown Elmer into her arms with the taxi idling next to us. He hadn't made a sound since I'd picked him up out of his cot.

I lay down with my back to my family. My mum whispered something to my dad.

I was surprised to find my hands meeting in front of my chest, and my own voice, a whisper:

Dead God, I hope you can hear me now. We haven't spoken before, because I don't believe in you, but this isn't about me, it's about Lasse. This is your chance to show me you exist. Lasse is going to be a dad for the second time, he still has so much to live for, we need him. Please, have mercy.

Minutes went by and nothing. Hours, then something.

Lasse's mum, brothers and sisters-in-law arrived. I'd been outside with my mum getting some air in a car park behind the hospital when, without warning, there they were in front of us.

We stood in the space between two cars, hugging each other in turn. They cried and cried, and I told them I'd been shocked at first too, but I knew now that Lasse would be all right.

The words came out of my mouth with such conviction I believed them myself. I even smiled.

If anyone can get through this, it's Lasse!

Was that laughter? It was. I'd laughed.

We'd be able to go into him soon. That must mean he'd stabilized. If he was going to die of this, it would have happened already. Now we were just waiting for him to wake up from his coma. Why else would they have moved him to intensive care?

We sat together in the waiting room. I got a plate with a mound of rice surrounded by a reddish-brown lake of meat. The rice was hard in the middle and I spooned the sauce over in an attempt to soften it. My sister-in-law Ina sat watching me with tears in her eyes. When I declared for the umpteenth time that I knew Lasse was going to make it, bits of reddish-brown rice flew out of my mouth and on to the table in front of me.

At some point in the afternoon, the doctor came to get me. Lasse's family stayed in the waiting room, but I wanted my mum with me. Out in the corridor the doctor asked me to stop for a second.

Was I sure I wanted to do this? Some people couldn't handle seeing their loved ones in such a state.

I assured him that I did, referred to myself as a *tough nut*. I'd worked at a nursing home when I was younger, I'd seen sick people before.

The doctor led us up a staircase and into a linoleum labyrinth with coloured lines painted along the floors, pulling cord after cord, causing the doors to spring open for us. We were heading towards the epicentre of the hospital, where beeps were tantamount to life.

I kept a brisk pace, carried the weight of my stomach in my arms.

I would speak to Lasse and he'd hear me, he'd hear me and decide to wake up. The adrenaline was pumping through my nervous system: *Bring it on!*

Then we were at the door. I went in first and my legs turned at once to jelly.

There he was. Lying motionless on a bed, a sheet covering him up to his shoulders, his naked body just about visible through the material. Various instruments were affixed to his temples and chest with suction cups. Cables connected him to other instruments displaying numbers I didn't know the meaning of. A nurse was standing next to the bed. She gave us a friendly nod but kept working, moving instruments around. His chest hair stuck to them. There were tubes that coiled around his head and disappeared under the sheet, reappearing at his feet. His lips were stretched around a thick, ribbed resuscitator that had been taped to his cheeks to hold it in place. It made his mouth large and lopsided. A garbled swallowing sound came from his throat.

Nnguh. Nnguh. Nnguh.

Why is he making that noise? I asked my mum.

The doctor answered, said it was a good sign, it meant he was trying to breathe by himself. I wanted to cover my ears, refuse to hear more.

Blood flowed from his nostrils and all the places where the needles pierced his skin.

The nurse pushed open one of his eyelids to see if his pupil would react to the light. I averted my eyes. She wrote down the result on a little pad of paper.

I looked at the pad, then at her.

Lasse uses contact lenses, I said, maybe you could take them out for him. It can't feel very nice with them drying up in there.

She opened his eyelids again and carefully removed the lenses. The way she spoke to him reminded me of the nursing home, the distant way I'd cared for people I didn't really know.

All right, Lasse, I'm just going to open your eyes and take out your contact lenses now. That should feel better. And the other. There we go, Lasse. That wasn't so bad, was it.

I hesitated, then reached out to touch him, stroked his forehead gently. It was freezing. It was all I could do not to snap my hand right back.

The doctor was telling my mum about the instruments and their various functions. He pulled the sheet aside to show her how they were attached. My husband lay stark naked before us, his penis limp and pulled to one side by a tube that ran from his urinary tract into a bag of urine hanging from the bed frame. There was a rectangular incontinence pad under his bum.

Mu-um! I exclaimed.

She couldn't just stand there looking at his dick! Up until now, his nakedness had belonged to him and me alone.

The doctor put the sheet back.

Someone wheeled a stool in and over to the bed, then saw me and came back with a chair I could actually sit on.

A steady stream of nurses and doctors bustled about, turning dials, writing things down and inspecting the drip feeds. There was an open door between Lasse's room and another room filled with screens and graphs and blinking lights and phones with muffled ringtones.

This was the moment I was supposed to open my mouth, but I felt suddenly embarrassed at the prospect of speaking intimately to him in the presence of so many people. I knew I had to say something so beautiful it would work better than all their medicine and machines.

His forehead was one of the few places free from tubes and blood, and I stroked it with the edge of my index finger as tears dripped from the tip of my nose. I stared at the blood trickling out of his ears.

I whispered that I was here now.

The rest of my words got stuck to the walls of my throat.

I had to press my fingers between his to hold his hand. He was beginning to swell up from all the liquid being pumped into him, his tongue took up more space and poked out between chapped lips, his neck was wider than usual. I was on high alert, watching for the slightest movement, the slightest sign of life.

My mouth was still open, but I couldn't think of anything else to say. Time was against us, he had to hear me.

The cold fingers, the swollen body, the blood running out of his nostrils, over his cheeks and down past his earlobes. It was my husband, lying there.

My husband, who, that very morning, had sung birthday songs to Elmer and insisted on porridge for breakfast because he'd read somewhere that porridge was the best thing to eat before a marathon. My husband, who, only a few days ago, had been discussing baby names with me. My husband, who'd hold me in his arms every night until I fell asleep.

But the words about life and love and us wouldn't come.

I tried.

I begged him to fight. Called him *my wounded warrior*, because I did that whenever he was sick and he loved it. I spoke in imperatives: *Wake up!* He had to, he had to be there for the birth of our second child. But when I heard myself thanking him for our children, I fell silent again. It sounded too much like goodbye. At a loss, I turned to face my mum and the nurse behind me.

I don't know what else to say, I said, I didn't come prepared with a speech or anything.

My mum laid a hand on my shoulder. I felt so inadequate.

That evening, the doctor called a family meeting out in the corridor. He took pains to look each of us in the eye in turn. It was something about Lasse's legs. They were stiff and they couldn't be stiff. Some specialists were on their way to assess the situation.

It didn't sound so bad. If they were spending time worrying about his legs, surely that meant there wasn't anything left to worry about with his head or his heart.

I found myself fast-forwarding to the likely rehabilitation period, a wheelchair probably, nothing we couldn't manage. But then I saw the looks on my in-laws' faces: wide-eyed and hands covering their mouths. All of them worked in the health service. They understood something about stiff legs that I didn't. In a tiny voice, Lasse's mum, Helle, asked about some specific values, a percentage of something in something.

The doctor cleared his throat and answered. Helle let out a gasp and fell sideways into Lasse's big brother, who just about managed to wrap his arm around her before she hit the floor.

But the tables could still turn, we had to keep the faith.

I kept the faith.

We were shown into another waiting area while the specialists examined Lasse. His two brothers sat curled up with their girlfriends.

My mum paced up and down the corridor, on the phone to my sisters in Copenhagen. Every so often she'd stop in her tracks and throw me a quick glance before covering her mouth and phone with her hand.

When is Dad coming? asked Lasse's little brother, Esben.

Helle was wringing her hands, strands of grey curls had escaped from her hairslide, the look in her eyes was wild.

He was at the airbase in Holland when I called him, so he's probably in Germany by now. One of his colleagues offered to drive him to Haderslev and drop him off at the house and then he'll drive our car the rest of the way here, but I told him he might as well go down to the cellar and hang up the wash I put on this morning, it's still sitting in the machine.

It looked as if something was fighting its way up the inside of her throat.

Why did I have to go and put that wash on? she whimpered.

We let her cry. My eyes met those of my sisters-in-law over the coffee table. We were thinking the same thing.

We spoke to each other in soft voices as the night slipped in through the window. My parents went to collect Elmer, taking him back to our apartment and leaving me outnumbered among Lasse's family: the two couples holding hands opposite me, and Helle, who'd soon have Hans by her side.

My friend Kira arrived, her hair pulled into a messy knot, woollen socks poking out of her trainers. She sat down next to me and put a hand on my back. I could feel the sweat from her palm through my top.

Kira was how Lasse and I had met. In gymnasium they had art class together twice a week, standing side by side in front of their enormous sketchpads. She painted chubby tortoises and threw him occasional sidelong glances. He painted a ferry sailing out of a chessboard, waves breaking on either side of it.

I sat cross-legged on a table behind them, struggling to pay attention to what Kira was saying. Lasse painted with such confidence – each brushstroke as sure and steady as the way he kept turning around to look at me was awkward and clumsy.

I couldn't stop thinking about him. I looked him up in the phonebook and found his parents' address. Next to the address: the family surname and the initials of their first names, among them the tiny L for Lasse. I gazed at the letter, enchanted. Never before had I been so taken with another person.

*

A bed was rolled out for me in a dark, quiet part of the corridor, but I refused to lie down and sleep. The night seemed to stretch out into eternity; the thought of waking up on the other side of it was unbearable.

I imagined telling Lasse the story of this night. I pictured him waking up with me by his side, and he would say, *The last thing I can remember is running*, and I would tell him the rest.

Around midnight, the doctor returned. He said that I could go in to Lasse again. I got up, my body weighing a thousand kilograms.

With every hour that passed, Lasse morphed before my eyes into something other. The more he swelled up, the more his features spread out, grew apart. Under the waxlike skin, his veins shimmered like a web of red and blue tacking thread. He was a body, breaking itself down.

His throat grew as wide as his thigh and, eventually, the swelling pushed his head so far back that it pointed his chin directly up at the ceiling, the beard he'd always kept so trim now a caricature of spiky bristles sticking out in all directions, his moustache dark and congealed with blood. All that remained was an abandoned shell, from which his soul had already taken flight.

It left in its wake a smell of sweat, sugary medicine and the plastic vacuum bags of tubes and needles and gauges the nurses kept ripping open, the smell of him merging with the smell of the room. He smelled of the flashing clamp on his index finger, of the doctor's green lab coat, of the computer in the corner.

My life was inextricably bound to his. We were one, or so I'd thought. But all I felt at the sight of this distorted body was disgust.

His hands were the only things I could bear to look at. And so I sat, staring at our interlaced fingers until they too grew so inflated I had to look away. I stared down at my shoes instead, willing myself to stay by his side but relieved when I was asked to leave the room.

I made one feeble attempt at protest, unwilling to accept my apparent willingness to give up so quickly, but the nurse said it would be best for the baby if I lay down for a bit. So I did. I left, the baby my excuse. And as soon as I did, I wished myself back again, couldn't bear being apart from him, couldn't bear the thought of him waking up right then, without me there.

Behind the white blinds, a jet-black night; beneath my eyelids, tiny grains of sand. I was ready to drop with fatigue, but still I felt undeserving of the luxury it was to climb out of my skirt and on to the bed, to prop my stomach up with a pillow and pull the blanket right up to my nose.

I dozed off into a choppy nightmare and, before I knew it, found myself tumbling back out of bed, the inside of my forehead prickling with vertigo, black spots obscuring my vision. I put a hand on the wall to steady myself, then staggered along the corridor in my leggings and pushed open the door to Lasse's room.

A yellowish light hung over Helle and Hans, who sat with furrowed brows, holding hands. Hans must have arrived while I was asleep.

Their faces said it all.

I bent over Lasse, stroked his forehead. The skin around his eyes was thick, his eyelids reduced to two thin lines that nearly swallowed his eyelashes whole. His tongue was even more swollen than before, his salivary glands bright red and pronounced, now bearing the imprint of his molars. The swallowing sound was no more.

Helle made to pass me something and I opened my palm automatically. Lasse's wedding ring.

Sorry, I'm sorry, I just had to take it off before, before he – She sobbed.

I looked at it, then at her. Felt my mouth hanging open, tears and snot sliding down my face and my heart thumping away inside, everything going impossibly slow, impossibly fast. I closed my fingers around it and tried to look up at Hans, my pupils darting in all directions. I blinked and his face became a blur, but behind his glasses I could still make out the desperation in his eyes.

You're somewhere else, where have you gone? he asked. I looked down at Lasse.

Helle implored me to try and sleep again. With laboured movements, I turned and left them, squeezing the ring in my hand. Maybe, somewhere deep in the tunnels of consciousness, Lasse could hear the echo of my steps, could hear I'd lost the faith, was leaving him. And maybe that was the moment he let himself get sucked down at last, down and out into eternity.

I fell into a deep, dreamless sleep, and when I woke, Helle was standing beside me. It was dark but I could tell by her breathing.

She was a mother who'd just lost a child.

Before going in to Lasse again, we were summoned to a meeting room. The light hurt my eyes. The doctor sat at the end of a conference table, the image of a blue pause button glowing on the wall behind him, cast by a projector someone had forgotten to turn off. *No external input.*

It wouldn't be ethical to keep Lasse artificially alive any

longer, said the doctor. His heart still hadn't started beating by itself; there was no activity in his brain.

My arms lay limp on the table before me. I was crying with my mouth open, surrounded by others doing the same: Kira, my mum, Lasse's family, all of them rocking in their chairs, hiding their faces in their hands.

I went in to see him first, dragging my feet in with me.

The nurses had retreated into the control room next door, the lights had been dimmed, he lay alone on the bed. A body that had long since given up, but now it had been said, words that couldn't be taken back.

I screamed. *I can't without Lasse.*

I don't remember if I said anything else, all I remember is the same sentence, over and over. I drooled, wiped my mouth and nose on the shoulder of my T-shirt and made to scream again when one of the nurses placed a hand on my shoulder. Gently, she turned me around to face her, her expression sympathetic.

Stand still for a moment.

I was panting, gasping for air.

She reached up to my forehead and removed a piece of paper towel that must have been stuck there the whole time we'd been in the meeting room with the doctor.

The others had already come in. I hadn't noticed them. It was too late, but there was still so much to say and do before they switched off the machines.

He has to hear Elmer's voice one last time, I pleaded, to no objections.

I couldn't bear the thought that he and the kids would never have the chance to say goodbye. It was my family, my responsibility.

I had some videos of Elmer on my phone, but my battery was long dead. I panicked, struggled to catch my breath.

What do we do now?

There was a computer in the corner of the room. Hans logged into Facebook and found a video Lasse had posted a month ago.

We couldn't figure out how to turn the volume up. It was hopeless.

The hospital priest had arrived and stood waiting, Bible in hand.

Lasse's nose kept up its watery trickle of blood. The nurses tried to locate the sound settings on the computer, but it was no use, we'd just have to keep quiet.

Trip, trap, trip, trap, trip, trap.

Elmer's bright little voice sounded low compared to the beeping of the machines. He was sitting at our dining table in his highchair, enthusiastically retelling the story of the three billy goats Gruff. We'd just eaten and his face shone with mashed potato and beetroot.

One billy goat after another went trip-trapping over the bridge. *Trip, trap,* they said as they went. There was Elmer Billy Goat, Cousin Neo Billy Goat, Grandma Billy Goat and Uncle Asbjørn Billy Goat. Elmer made it up to ten billy goats, the troll growling at every one of them:

Who's that! Trip-trapping! Bridge!

He was trembling in excitement, gleefully punching the air with clenched fists as he spoke.

The film panned over to me. Lasse was filming, watching me through the lens. I was smiling, August-tanned and round with pregnancy, my chin resting in my hands, elbows on the table.

What about Dad Billy Goat? asked Lasse.

We laughed.

Lasse's hand appeared on screen from the right; he patted Elmer on the shoulder.

Thanks for the story, Elmer.

Elmer grinned in delight.

Cut, said Lasse.

Cut, said Elmer.

They turned the computer off.

The hospital priest opened a window so that Lasse's soul could fly out.

I lay down next to him on the bed and clung to his legs through the sheet, as the others began to sing:

We thank him now with joyful song / For all that he has given / For fields that grew all summer long / For word and life from heaven.

It was beautiful, intimate, remote. Voices wobbling, rising and falling, breaking, the priest the only one of us able to hold the tune.

Then it was time. To switch off the machines. They turned so many dials and pushed so many buttons I couldn't figure out which were the deciding ones.

But it didn't matter. Everything that had ever been Lasse was already gone.

III

It was Lasse's first half-marathon. Elmer and I stood cheering from the pavement around the five-kilometre mark, surrounded by flags and shouting *go, go, go* and *you can do it* with all the other spectators.

The front runners flew by in their skin-tight shorts and breathable T-shirts, their feet a drumroll on the asphalt.

Lasse ended up somewhere in the thronging middle, coming into sight at the end of the road in his new running shoes, his shorts flapping about his thighs, his eyes scanning the crowd until they found us and lit up.

There's Dad! Hi Dad! I yelled. Lasse waved, then he'd passed us.

Elmer wriggled down from my hip, tried to run after him.

Elmer run with Dad! he cried, stomping so enthusiastically I had to squat down to keep hold of him in the crowd.

Sorry, Elmer, you can't. Dad's running very fast, and he's got a long way to go, a long, long way up and down lots of hills and around a lake. It's too far for you.

There were tears welling up in my eyes, but I wiped them away before anyone saw. Put them down to pregnancy, oversensitivity, all the people, Lasse's pride, Elmer's devotion to his dad.

Pernille stood a few metres behind us, and when I turned around, she grinned and raised her phone in the air to say she'd taken the photo. I gave her a thumbs-up with my free hand, Elmer hanging on to the other.

A day and a half later I took his hand again, led him into his bedroom and closed the door behind us. I'd just come home from the crisis counsellor's and our apartment was still teeming with people.

In Elmer's bedroom it was quiet.

I asked him to sit with me on the racing-track mat and he flopped down, his nappy making a little *puf* sound.

On the wall was the giant elephant poster Lasse had made for Elmer: a grid of A4 sheets of paper, printed out and glued together. They'd begun to peel away from each other, so the elephant's trunk was now swollen and wonky.

Elmer looked up at me with serious eyes.

I asked him if he could remember that Dad was out running and that he had a long way to go?

Yes, he said, expectantly.

Well, Dad had to run really, really far, and he ran so far that he made it all the way up into the sky, so high up that he couldn't get down again. That's where he is now. He's sitting on a star, watching over us. The star is a long, long way from here, which is why we can't see him, but he can still see us.

Elmer looked and looked and looked at me.

Dad's moved on to the star, that's where he lives now. He doesn't live with us any more, and he won't be coming home again, little man, not ever, I said, my tears about to strangle me.

The photo of Lasse from the half-marathon was lying face down in my lap, and now I turned it over and waved to Lasse.

Bye-bye, Dad.

Elmer copied me, waved and said bye-bye, and then he patted the photo of the person who until now had constituted half of his very foundation, but who from now on would fade to nothing more than a memory.

There there, Dad, he said, and I pulled him into me and kissed him on the head, my tears falling into his white-blonde hair, wetting it flat.

Then he stood up and turned to face me, so our eyes were level. I tried to decode his expression. He wasn't crying, just looking at me quizzically.

Mum's mouth is crying. Elmer wipe mouth, he said.

His face concentrated, he began to dab at my mouth, my cheeks, my eyes.

I had planned for us to sit on the balcony when it got dark, thinking I'd find a nice twinkly star for Lasse and teach Elmer to wave goodnight to him.

But it was cloudy. The stars had betrayed us, and I betrayed Elmer when I tucked him up in his cot and closed the door to his room. I was so exhausted I could barely stand. I needed to be alone.

I woke to the dark of the bedroom in the middle of the night, the apartment finally silent. My big sister lay curled up next to me with Lasse's duvet pulled over her head. I rolled out of bed, switched on the light and stumbled over to the laundry basket, burrowed down through the layers of dirty clothes in search of something, anything, that still smelled of him; something, anything, that could bring him back, even if just for a moment.

At the bottom of the pile I found a black cotton T-shirt, a hint of his skin in the fibres. I pressed my face into it. Sweet oil, clay and scalp, a whiff of Hugo Boss, but the smell was already waning. I had to find a way to hold on to him.

I pulled the T-shirt over my pillow, turned it into a male torso for me to rest my head on. Nicoline had woken up; she put her arm around me and I pushed her away.

By morning my tears had cleansed the T-shirt of all remaining traces of Lasse. I pressed my nose into the armpits like a desperate truffle pig, but he was gone.

In the bathroom, I splashed my puffy face with cold water. I didn't want Elmer to see me crying so early in the day, but every time I dried my eyes with the towel, new tears had already begun to form. The lump in my throat felt like an infection.

Nicoline was tiptoeing around the kitchen, trying to find things for breakfast, but I wanted to take care of everything involving Elmer myself. He was my child, my responsibility. I got out the usual bowls, the porridge, raisins, milk, Elmer's bib – this I could do.

We ate breakfast amid the nauseating stench of lilies.

Lasse had been dead for twenty-four hours and we were already inundated with bouquets. My cafetière was full of lilies, as was the plastic container we used for the blender: we'd run out of vases. All of a sudden I couldn't stomach the sight of flowers. Soon to decay in foul-smelling water, all those extra trips down to the bins in the backyard.

I sat on the floor in the hall with Elmer on my lap, unable to dress him while standing because of my stomach. He tried to break free when I pulled the anorak Lasse's mum had made for him over his head. I crawled over to the shoes and wiggled them on to his feet, pulling my own shoes on as he ran back into the apartment. I rolled on to my hands and knees and pushed myself up from the floor, caught Elmer and carried him down the stairs to where the pushchair was waiting for us. It bumped against the door frame as I tried to manoeuvre it out of the building, down the stone steps and on to the pavement, the door hitting my elbow as it slammed shut behind us.

Sunglasses on to conceal my raw eyes, I set off in a hurry, pushing the pushchair mechanically in front of me.

Elmer was pointing at all the cars driving by.

Beep beep! he cried in delight, as if every car was the first he'd ever seen.

Mmm, beep beep, I replied, my jaw clenched. I just had to make it to nursery without falling apart.

I parked the pushchair outside, unstrapped Elmer and took his hand. We were heading for the cloakroom when one of the other mothers came towards us, smiling her big white teeth.

Big day today!

I frowned, causing my eyebrows to rub against the frame of my sunglasses. In the silence that followed, she persisted, still smiling:

Oh, my bad, isn't it today he turns two?

I'd forgotten.

I couldn't hold back the tears back any longer. I tore my sunglasses off and stood helplessly with them in one hand and the birthday boy in the other. He didn't say a word.

That evening we held a sombre party. Helle brought a cake, poked two candles in it and lit them at the dining table, where Elmer sat in his highchair.

I'd only invited family, but a seemingly endless stream of mine and Lasse's friends trickled into the apartment bearing enormous presents for Elmer and even more flowers. He was a toddler surrounded by a mob of sympathetic faces. There were cups of coffee and napkins everywhere. Our guests took turns locking themselves in the bathroom and patting each other on the back when they emerged again.

I sat on a chair next to Elmer and helped him with the cake.

Someone asked me if we had more teaspoons. Forks, then?

Did I want another cup of coffee?

What I wanted was to leap to my feet and scream at them to

get the fuck out of my home. I wanted to be alone with Elmer on the racing-track mat beneath the elephant poster.

How about we sing a birthday song for Elmer? my dad suggested to the living room, and it annoyed me that he always had to take charge, even now.

'Today It Is Elmer's Birthday' – what about that one? he asked Elmer, who looked excitedly from guest to guest as they put their teaspoons back down on their plates, wiped their mouths and cleared their throats.

Today it is Elmer's birthday, we began. So far so good. But when we got to *Mum and Dad are waiting at home*, we avoided making eye contact with each other.

At *May Elmer live forever more and get everything he wishes for*, I had to give up.

The doctor had said that no one could understand how an otherwise fit and healthy twenty-seven-year-old man could go into heart failure just like that, or why they hadn't been able to restart his heart afterwards. It would take months for the autopsy to reveal whether Lasse had suffered from a heart condition he might have passed on to our children.

The song finished and I chimed in with an unconvincing *hurrah*.

Life is full of windows that you pass without seeing until, all of a sudden, you're standing in front of one and it's meant for you. I must have walked by the undertaker's on the way to Elmer's nursery every morning and afternoon for the past year or so, but I'd barely registered its existence. Lasse probably hadn't either.

The carpet was dark green, and the same photo of a watering can filled with wild flowers hung in the reception area and the meeting room to the side.

I shook the undertaker's hand and unzipped my raincoat. I could still just about close it over my stomach. It had been raining heavily all night and morning, and when I hung my coat up, a little puddle began to form on the floor beneath it.

Lasse's family were already there, sitting at a round table in silence, waiting for me.

The undertaker brought out two enormous ring binders full of photos of flowers, urns and coffins. We were to decide which were 'most Lasse'.

A bizarre decision to make on his behalf. Lasse was an architect. Unlike me, he had an eye for aesthetics, and I knew it would actually matter to him what his coffin looked like. If it had been me in his place, you could have put me a plain wooden box with a dandelion on top for all I cared.

Those are supposed to be nice, and *what about those?* Helle and I said to each other, flipping through the pages of funeral sprays. I was waiting for the perfect arrangement to jump out from the page, to manifest itself in all its rightness.

The undertaker sat with us. He listened patiently as we, talking over each other, described what had happened; as we launched into anecdotes about Lasse and fell silent as abruptly as we'd started. He kept listening when Helle said her sister had also lost a son far too young. He shook his head kindly when Hans pulled out his credit card, said *later*. He nodded along as I held my stomach and assured him I was happy I had another child on the way, and I'd make it work, even though I knew it wasn't going to be easy. Words I'd repeated too many times to count in the past twenty-four hours.

Eventually, the undertaker's face crumpled. He removed his glasses, wiped his forehead and apologized. Sometimes it was difficult to keep a professional distance, he said.

The rain rolled down the window facing out to the street, the steam of our breath making everything outside blurry.

The undertaker asked me to stop by later that day with the clothes Lasse would wear in his coffin. I pulled the hood of my raincoat over my hair and said goodbye to my in-laws. I didn't hug them.

On the way home the rain flooded my shoes and socks, water squelching out of the small air holes with every step.

My abdomen suddenly jolted, going into a succession of what I hoped were false contractions.

The funeral was planned for Saturday. That was the first thing to get through. Beyond that I couldn't think.

Out of breath, I climbed the stairs to our apartment on the second floor, not looking at the nameplate with our three names on it as I let myself in. I had barely slept for three days and, in my depleted state, the most basic of movements had me gasping for air.

I slid the wardrobe door open to reveal two dust covers, hanging side by side. I took care not to touch the one containing my wedding dress.

Lasse's hands had hung up the suit he wore for our wedding; now my hands took it down and unzipped the dust cover, mirroring his movements.

I removed the shirt and trousers, but left the smoking jacket on the hanger. Maybe some day the boys would want to try on their dad's smartest jacket, feel the span of his shoulders, how handsome he'd felt.

I folded the trousers and shirt neatly and arranged them on top of each other in the nicest paper bag I could find in the kitchen. Then took it all out again and put his leather shoes at the bottom. It wouldn't do for him to be laid to rest in a white shirt with shoeprints all over it. I placed his light blue bow tie and the watch with the orange strap on top. He loved that watch. We'd spent a long time in the shop in New York choosing it together.

Without knowing exactly what I was looking for, I found his wallet and rifled through it. Tucked between all his cards was a little scrap of paper.

Bra 34A. Knickers 38.

Lasse's handwriting: his particular way of writing each letter from the bottom up. He must have written it before I got pregnant again.

I felt the muscles in my legs releasing of their own accord, sliding me down on to the floor, the note clutched to my chest.

My man, no more.

He trod hard on my toes with his high-vis running shoes as he leaned in to kiss me goodbye. We were standing in the doorway to our apartment; he was about to leave for his half-marathon.

Oww, for fuck's sake, I exclaimed.

He pursed his lips and took a deep breath through his nose. Looked at me for a moment, a tiny shake of his head, then disappeared down the stairs, already running late.

We'd had a fight.

The kiss was supposed to make up for it.

Four days later, I got a call from Lasse's big brother Christian. There was something I ought to know. He took a deep breath.

Lasse was in the papers.

Hans and Helle had contacted a local journalist about what had happened. Then a national tabloid had picked up the tragic story about the twenty-seven-year-old runner who'd mysteriously collapsed and died, and the source close to him who wanted to speak about it. They'd called Helle back.

I hung up and opened my laptop, found the articles.

They'd used a photo of him they must have taken from his Facebook profile; his half-open mouth and lowered gaze made it look like he was mourning. I knew he was looking down at Elmer in his arms, but they'd cropped that out.

The heat rushed to my cheeks as I read. Helle had told them about Lasse, about me and Elmer. She'd given them my name and his, described the pregnant wife at home in the kitchen getting ready for 'little Elmer's' birthday party.

It was a story fit for violins. There they were, the violins, playing, and here I was, having neither been asked nor heard. I was furious.

Lasse's death was nobody's fault. But the mere feeling – of anger, of having someone to blame – felt like relief, like my body letting go: a boil bursting, pus rushing out.

The closer we got to the funeral, the more intense the pain in my abdomen became. A sharp metal hand had wrapped itself around my womb and was pulling down, hard. The pain merged with my longing for Lasse, until I couldn't differentiate between the baby's kicks and the kicking of my own grief.

I was carrying a dead man's child, and it felt like every breath I took could be my last too.

A child is hooked up to its mother's circulatory system, and I'd read that mother and child's feelings are also entwined in a tight web of symbiosis. When a mother feels joy, so does her baby, which made my grief a poison I was unrelentingly pumping into him, which made me anxious, made me panic. Inside me wasn't a safe place to be right now, but the alternative wasn't pretty either: if my body started sounding the alarm, it could kick-start the birth.

It was far too early, he wasn't ready. Nor was I.

I rang Skejby Hospital's maternity ward.

I'm twenty-six weeks along, I said. My husband died on Monday. I'm scared I haven't been taking proper care of the baby. I'm scared he might be dead.

*

Two hours later, my mum was driving me to Skejby's ultra-sound clinic for an emergency scan. When we drove past the entrance to the cardiac unit I averted my eyes, gritted my teeth.

Four days ago.

A doctor ushered us past the waiting area and directly into a private room, gestured for me to stand on the scales. He consulted my medical record: I'd lost weight since last time, when I ought to have gained it. It was crucial I started eating again, he said, then asked us to wait while he went to fetch the handheld scanner.

I kicked off my shoes, pulled myself on to the examination table and lay on my back, staring at the ceiling. My mum sat down on a chair beside me. I could just about see her out of the corner of my eye.

Mum, did you know that the end of the world will be on the 21st of December this year? It's something to do with the Mayan calendar. People think the last date in the Mayan calendar is a prediction for the end of the world. That'll be right after I've given birth, if all goes to plan.

My due date was the 10th of December. Exactly three months after Lasse's death.

I turned my head and my mum met my gaze, her eyes pink and puffy. She looked older than usual: white flyaway hair, a deep line between her eyebrows.

She and Lasse had been close. Unlike the rest of us, she stuck around for his monologues about architectural masterpieces and how much he hated glazed tiles, kit homes and anything too flashy, long after everyone else had given up. The two of them would stay at the dining table talking into the night, as the rest of us turned up the music and danced into the living room, the way my family had always done after a hearty meal. Lasse was a clumsy dancer but an unstoppable talker. She must have missed him terribly too.

Not that I'm superstitious or anything, I said, but it did used to worry me, the end of the world, the idea that we'd all disappear. Now it feels more like relief. Freedom.

The ceiling above me was trembling.

It's not like I have a choice. I have the kids, I'm all they have left now, and I'll keep going for their sake, but if it wasn't up to me, if it just happened and we all disappeared at once? Well, I think it would be nice to let go of all that responsibility. I've already lost everything there is to lose.

I blinked; the ceiling calmed down.

I hadn't needed my mum like this since I was a child. I waited for her to comfort me or tell me to pull myself together, tell me that my children might be my responsibility but I was hers, and she wasn't about to let the world end on her watch.

That's how you feel now, she said. I know it's impossible to imagine, but that's not how you're always going to feel. This too shall pass.

By the time the doctor returned with the scanner, we were waiting in silence. He asked me to lift my top up, then squeezed a blob of cold gel on to my distended stomach and carefully pressed the scanner to my skin, letting it glide from my pubic bone up to my navel.

Right away, the baby materialized on the screen. Alive and kicking and apparently just having woken up from a nap – he was yawning his funny little alien mouth and wiping his nose. He tried to stretch his arms and legs out, and now I could place the movements inside me: not kicks of grief but of the little feet on the screen. I burst into laughter.

The world was still here – as was I – kicking away. I felt hungry again.

I'd lost, but I hadn't lost everything.

My card was declined in Føtex. Protocol, apparently, when you have a joint account and one of you dies: they block everything, just in case the widow tries to jet off to Bali with a suitcase stuffed full of cash.

I called the bank and they asked me to come in to reopen my account and increase my overdraft.

Lasse's architect salary was the only reason we could afford a two-bedroom apartment in the city centre, the only way we'd ever be able to provide for a second child. I was still studying to be a journalist, my income consisted solely of student grants, and I had two semesters to go. I'd been one week into my internship at Århus Stiftstidende when Lasse died.

My financial situation was hopeless. My dad had called my insurance company. He stood slumped over in our living room as he relayed the news that there was nothing they could do to help. It was the first time I'd ever seen him cry.

My grandparents had given me five thousand kroner to buy Elmer and myself some new clothes for the funeral.

In the days immediately after Lasse's death, I couldn't have cared less that the utter mess I was was on display for all to see. But now, five days later and the day before the funeral, I decided to do something about my appearance. From this moment on it would become a matter of principle for me to look presentable at all times.

A few weeks earlier, I'd been eyeing up a pair of leather boots but hadn't bought them. We couldn't afford it, Lasse had said. He'd been the financially responsible one of the two of us, keeping track of our food budget and savings account. Now we were just me.

I bought the boots without even trying them on. My mum carried the bag for me as we made our way to Matas for a waterproof mascara. Then to GANNI, where I asked to see everything that was black, elegant and pregnancy-compatible. I bought a short dress with a cord that tied under my breasts and a pair of black tights with a back seam. Then to Magasin to find something for Elmer.

We were rifling through a rack of shirts when a shop assistant asked if we needed any help. She almost jumped when we looked up with our tear-streaked faces, but quickly recovered her composure.

We're looking for something a two-year-old can wear to a funeral, said my mum.

Boy or girl? asked the shop assistant, leading us over to the section for wealthy people, toddler suits lined up on little wooden hangers.

We found a pair of grey corduroy trousers, a grey checked shirt and a navy woollen waistcoat to go with it. We nodded our acquiescence. It was too expensive, but we didn't have the strength to keep looking.

Unless you'd prefer something all in black? asked the shop assistant.

No, no, he's not the one who died, I answered a bit too quickly. Thank God.

The shop assistant and my mum stared at me. We paid as fast as we could and hurried out of the shop.

I stood before the full-length mirror in the bedroom and got dressed as slowly as humanly possible. I had an hour and a half to kill before the funeral and was determined to fill every second of it with some kind of activity. I knew that if I gave myself the slightest chance to feel anything, I wouldn't last the day.

The bedroom was warm, but my fingers were purple and my hands were shaking.

I ought to have been practising the speech I'd written the day before, but I couldn't bring myself to look at the words I'd planned to say to Lasse. It was enough to have to do it once.

I fastened my bra in the right hook and rolled my tights up and over my stomach, but they wouldn't stretch far enough, so I pulled them back down to my hips. I took my new dress off its hanger and held the neck open as I lowered it carefully over my hairsprayed head.

Then I found the thin gold chain Lasse had given me back when we lived in New York. I clasped it around my neck.

My mum knocked on the door and asked if it was time for Elmer to get dressed.

I answered that I wanted to do it myself. Another fifteen minutes taken care of.

I turned my back to the mirror to see the dress from behind. It was far too short. With my arms raised to shoulder height, it crept right up under my bum. The very visible seams down the backs of my legs didn't help. I called for my parents.

They found other pairs of tights, all either full of holes or too small. My dad opened my wardrobe and pulled out some old dresses, which my mum and I immediately rejected. Eventually, my dad cut the legs off a pair of leggings with kitchen scissors so I could wear them as shorts under my dress.

I studied my reflection – red-eyed, black-clad, thigh-length – and tried to comfort myself with the thought that, if Lasse was watching over us, he wouldn't be able to resist me.

Aarhus Cathedral was a mere ten-minute walk from our apartment. The pushchair bumped along over the cobblestones and I clung to it to prevent myself from keeling over. Elmer bumped along with it, quietly handsome in his new outfit, a layer of drizzle covering our coats and hair.

Soon enough, the downcast faces of friends and family came into view. They moved forward to greet me, but I strode wordlessly past them and into the church.

Flower wreaths lined the aisle all the way to the altar, in pink, white, red, orange. Gold writing on white ribbons, young people dressed in black, high heels on stone floors, coats being unzipped, an overwhelming smell of freshly cut stems. I held my breath and parked the pushchair, picked Elmer up and hugged him close to me.

The undertaker was there, wanting my opinion on something

to do with the cards on the wreaths. I just shook my head and walked past him. Made for the coffin and its exuberance of flowers – the funeral spray we must have chosen.

But there were people everywhere. Everyone touching my arm, wanting to *be there* for me. Even after I reached my chair, they queued up to offer their condolences, embrace me fiercely, murmur words I could only agree with.

He was. It is.

Their cold fingers on my stomach, on Elmer's head. My cheek growing clammy with foundation and aftershave, my dress absorbing their overpowering perfume.

I had my back to Lasse as I spoke to them, and all I wanted was to turn and go to him – my patience, my politeness, had all but run out. I sent my dad a look and he intervened, shepherded them all away.

I folded myself over the coffin, rested my cheek on the cold wood and wept over Lasse. It didn't feel good, but it felt right. My breath made little dull patches on the sleek mahogany.

The organ began to play and I pushed myself up from the coffin, sat back on the chair with Elmer on my lap. The same priest who married Lasse and I just two and a half years ago now stood to deliver his eulogy. He used the word *senseless* and it was the most sense I'd heard all week.

Elmer couldn't sit still. He soon slid off my lap and went tottering about among the wreaths, bending over and picking all the largest flower heads for me. His new trousers kept sliding down, his bright green boxer shorts on display to the entire congregation.

After the hymns I got up to make my speech. I mumbled some nonsense about how it was like we knew that Sunday morning would be our last together. I said the truth:

67

You taught me how to live. Now I need that more than ever.

The priest returned with the silver bucket and everyone stood. He scooped a little heap of soil up and on to the coffin.

From earth you have come, he said.

We were silent. Save for a few subdued sniffles.

To earth you shall return, the priest continued.

He dipped the trowel into the bucket again; I felt my throat constrict, tears welling up. And then Elmer, pointing and beaming at the soil on top of the coffin:

It's coffee!

His voice bouncing off the walls.

Offee, offee!

And so I found myself, midway through my husband's funeral, trying to swallow back laughter, as the priest concluded:

And from earth you shall rise again.

I dreamed I was in Føtex.

Shopping for dinner for two, an adult and a child. I put a little salmon fillet in my basket.

It's not enough, Lasse said.

I shook my head and kept going. He followed.

In the fruit and veg section I put a punnet of cherry tomatoes in my basket. He was getting agitated now, I could sense him behind me. I took a little handful of spaghetti.

It's not enough for me as well, he cried out in desperation.

Now he was standing behind me.

I turned and poked him in the stomach with the dried spaghetti. He popped silently, like a bubble.

You're not here any more, I whispered.

IV

Monday, two days after the funeral, I woke up to the void, lying on my side and contemplating Lasse's duvet on his side of the bed. I didn't want to spend one more minute awake.

Elmer was calling out for me, but when I went into his room and tried to pick him up, he didn't want me to. He didn't want me to stay and he didn't want me to leave. I picked him up anyway and he hit me, eyes ablaze.

After a breakfast of crying and screaming, I carried him into the hall to get him dressed. I needed him at nursery so I could break down in peace. I'd set my mental clock – I knew exactly how long I had to hold myself together.

He fought with all his might against his coat and shoes, lying on the floor and kicking every time I tried to touch him. I had to grab hold of his ankles for fear he might strike my stomach.

Hey little man, what's all the fuss? I said, trying to keep my voice calm. Not that you could hear it over all the screaming.

Another kick, my hand still around his ankle, sent pain shooting up through my elbow and into my shoulder.

I carried him squirming down the stairs and held him in one arm as I opened the main door with my foot and pulled the pushchair out. Once on the street, I strapped Elmer in and

73

walked as fast as I could in the direction of nursery, him scream-
ing and throwing his weight about in the pushchair, passers-by
giving us funny looks.

An ambulance flew by. I winced.

Lasse, lying lifeless on a stretcher in his torn running gear. I
hadn't been there, so why was that image so clear? I shook my
head frantically: *Get it out, not now, not yet, nursery first.*

I took a shortcut down a little street of old townhouses. The
entrance to Elmer's nursery was located up some sloping stone
steps between two tall hedges. I was trembling as I lifted him
screaming out of the pushchair so I could drag it up the steps.

There you go, chick, I said, now you –

But he drowned me out, and I'd already forgotten my next
words. He slumped down on the pavement, snot dribbling from
his nostrils.

My jaw clenched in panic.

Elmer!

As I raised my voice, I saw that I was holding my arms out
in front of me without any idea of what I'd been planning to use
them for. Never before had I felt so powerless over my own
child. He was unreachable.

As if by magic, an elderly woman appeared beside us. Short
grey hair and golden skin and white laughter lines around her
eyes. She spoke directly to Elmer, who was gazing up at her.

Hello down there, she said, I was just going to pick some
flowers in my garden, do you want to come and help? I live right
here, see, she said, pointing around the hedge.

From where I stood, I could make out a lawn ringed by tall
bushes, a loaded plum tree in the middle.

Elmer stopped crying and stood up, wiping his eyes.

Can you open the gate by yourself?

He pushed his whole body up against it until it swung open. Before following him in, the woman turned to me and reassured me that the situation was under control. Her kindness was too much. I burst into tears.

Sorry, it's just that . . . Åhh, it's such a mess! My husband died a week ago. I don't know . . .

A flicker of something darted across her face, then was gone. I hiccupped.

Take it easy. Just wait here and catch your breath, I'll look after him.

She took Elmer's hand and together they walked over to the bed of flowers at the back of the garden. She let him pick every single one. He pointed at the plum tree and she nodded and disappeared for a moment, returning with a plastic bag.

I dried my eyes on my sleeve and went after them into the garden.

Elmer ran beaming over to me and thrust the bag, now full of plums, into my hand. The woman gave him the flowers.

Thank you. I don't know what to say.

No need to say anything. Do you have people helping you?

I nodded.

Plenty.

Elmer pulled at my coat and she laughed indulgently.

Now look who's in a hurry!

They waved to each other as he marched up the steps to the nursery, clutching the flowers. I followed him, the bag of plums bouncing up and down on the pushchair.

At night I begged. I bargained with the darkness and implored the stars to return him to me. When they didn't answer, I howled my despair into his pillow. The sun rose on me whimpering my requests out into the empty bedroom.

I put his glasses on and cried into his contact-lens case, stroked his coffee percolator, got out all his notebooks and read every single page. His sentences drove me mad: *In one corner the wall is not curved, but faceted, creating sharp shadows instead of a gradient.* Were they his own words or something he'd copied down from a lecture? What was I hoping to find anyway?

And the photo of him, now crumpled from having accompanied me everywhere – I sat gazing at it in the hope that I might provoke something, anything, a moment in which his face would come alive again, miraculously wink at me from the afterlife, say: *You know I'm breaking ALL the rules by doing this, right?* And that alone would be enough to sustain me for the rest of my life.

Our kitchen was empty. I had scoured the fridge and cupboards, hoping for a little bit of pasta or leftover sausage I could scrape together into some semblance of dinner, a loud bang for every cupboard door I slammed shut.

I took a deep breath through my nose, puffed up my cheeks and blew slowly out of my mouth. I was exhausted and there was still so much evening to get through before I could collapse on the sofa.

I called for Elmer, who was already in his pyjamas, and said we had to go to Kvickly.

Wellies and a woollen jumper over the top would have to do. We walked hand in hand through the mild evening togethers. I looked down at him and thought: I could be happy if I wasn't so unhappy. His steps were so tiny compared to mine. He chatted away as we walked and my heart went out to him.

In the shop I picked Elmer up so he could see down into the freezer. Hawaiian pizza it was, and he wanted to carry the box to the till himself. He bore it proudly through the aisles and the cashier smiled first at him, then at me, as he stood on his tiptoes and pushed the box on to the belt. I returned her smile with a lump in my throat. Wished I could see him the way she did, wished I could treasure our alone time now that we were so rarely just the two of us, wished I could buy a pizza without guilt, wished his bedtime would hurry up and arrive.

One morning I sat on the living-room floor scratching my thighs, my fingers moving quickly and of their own accord. I wondered if I could dig so deep I'd be able to reach my feelings, and scratch a hole in them so they could spill out too.

I laid off.

Knew that if my skin became infected, it would stand little chance of healing while I was pregnant and fluid-swollen. Knew it could harm the baby.

Fuck! I wailed, clenching my nails into my fists and beating them against my thighs, still at a reasonable distance from my stomach so I wouldn't risk hitting it. I could feel my thigh bones under my skin – the fluids, the flesh, they shook, the pain felt good, but what if the baby felt it too?

I stopped myself mid-punch, let out a final despairing wail and lay myself carefully down on one side, cradling my stomach in both hands.

If I could just stay still, here, like this, nothing could harm us.

I wanted to forget everything, wanted to drink myself out of my mind, delete Lasse and responsibility and pregnancy and disappear to India without my phone, take acid on a beach until it rained and the rain washed the wet sand into my mouth, my nostrils, my eyes, turning to quicksand and sinking me with it, swallowing me whole. I thought about suicide. I didn't think I wanted to kill myself, but what if thinking it was the first step on the way to doing it? And what about the kids?

I wept over my own undoing, its inescapability – every escape attempt thwarted before it even got going, because, deep down, I knew there was no way I was ever going to trade my shitty life for anything else.

Despite our youth, Lasse and I had spoken a lot about death, about what we'd do if one of us died before it was time. I was usually the one who brought it up. I had a thing for existential discussions; I loved the thrill of hovering over the abyss, toes sticking out over the edge as I peered into its depths, Lasse holding my hand all the while.

A few years before the half-marathon, I'd read a heartbreaking story in a magazine about messengers from the afterlife, about a woman convinced her recently deceased husband had returned to her as a sparrow. She'd entered her living room one day to find the bird, sitting there unperturbed and seemingly at home. She'd spoken to it and shed a few tears before opening the window to let it fly away.

There was a photo of her gazing out of the window, dressed in a crocheted top, her hair loose and chestnut brown. More photos of her with a set of pink crystals. At the time I remember thinking if you were the kind of person who believed in crystals, it probably increased the chances of your husband turning into a sparrow. But still the idea stuck with me.

I told Lasse about it and suggested we make a pact: if it turned out to be possible to send a message from the great beyond, then the one who died would do everything within their power to do so. And the one left behind would mobilize all their senses to receive the message in whatever form it might take. A heart-shaped cloud, a bird, a butterfly – ideally, a ghost in human form, but if that turned out not to be possible . . .

Lasse thought I was silly and cute, and we shook on it.

In the wake of his death, I searched high and low for signs. Midway through washing up I caught myself staring absent-mindedly out of the window at a gull, studying its every movement – if only I could crack the code, figure out what it was trying to say, if it was trying to say *I miss you too*. But when it flew down to the bins in the backyard, instead of over to my windowsill, I came to my senses, ashamed to find myself hands-deep in soapy water thinking that a black-headed gull might have been able to repair my broken heart.

The day we interred Lasse's ashes, there was a bee.

We buried the urn on an unusually beautiful day in late September. Finally, a break in the rain, the air fresh in our lungs, the sky clear blue, the windflowers around the gravestones swaying in the breeze and the heart-shaped leaves of the katsura trees aflame.

I'd invited a few close friends and family to the ceremony. Elmer was at nursery. The plan was to meet at the chapel to collect the urn, then walk together down to the burial plot at the end of the avenue.

We spoke in low voices as we waited for the last guests to arrive. All of us decked out in dark coats and sunglasses, the flowers in our hands the only source of colour. I'd brought Purple Heart calla lilies – the same kind that had filled my bridal bouquet and Lasse's buttonhole. I gave them to my dad to carry.

When everyone was gathered, I went into the chapel alone. A woman in a suit pushed open the heavy door to the room which held the urn.

Daylight broke into colourful shards through the stained-glass windows. The door closed behind me as I walked a few paces forward with bated breath. On a table up against the far wall: the black urn.

I rested my hands on its cold surface and didn't know what to feel, other than the knot in my chest that by now had made a permanent home in me. My mouth opened but couldn't conjure a single word. I knew my voice would only make the situation creepy, or comical, and this was a place of quiet.

I picked up the urn and hugged it to my chest, balanced it on my stomach. Surprisingly heavy.

As I stepped out of the chapel I could hear the hum of a bee close by. If there is such a thing as a friendly bee, this one was it. It circled me calmly, seemingly uninterested in anyone else, even though they were carrying flowers that ought to have enticed it. I kept my gaze trained on the bee and felt a strange allegiance to it, despite being allergic to bee stings.

On our way down the avenue it disappeared.

The urn was a struggle to carry, my stomach tightening as we walked, my feet aching. I was regretting the decision to wear my new heeled boots.

A deep, cylinder-shaped hole had been dug at the burial plot. Two men in overalls stood waiting for us, each leaning on a spade, heads bowed. The woman in the suit tied a white ribbon around the urn so I could lower it into the damp earth.

I crouched down and the bee was back, hovering calmly

beside me. It crossed my mind how ridiculous it would be to get stung right there and then, as I solemnly interred my husband's urn. The bee landed on my thigh and I didn't bat it away.

We cast flowers into the hole, then the men began to shovel the soil back in, patting it level.

We sang a hymn and the bee stayed until the last line, then took off.

I watched until it vanished into the blue.

Whether a message had been sent or not, it had been received.

Lasse had been running under a tree when he fell.

A man called to fill in the part of the story I'd been missing.

He'd been the first to administer CPR, he told me over the phone, his deep voice breaking as he spoke. He was a paramedic, but that Sunday he'd been out running the half-marathon too, and had spotted Lasse, lying face down on the side of the road close to the twenty-kilometre mark – nearly ran right past him.

You OK, mate?

He'd rolled Lasse on to his back and Lasse had let out a little *puh*, his eyes closed. The man had immediately begun CPR, and after a few minutes he was joined by another runner, a cardiologist, but they couldn't get Lasse's heart to beat by itself. Fuck! the paramedic had shouted.

He shouted it again when he saw the background image on Lasse's phone – Elmer – and the running app still counting seconds as it lay next to his lifeless body.

I'd hoped for silver linings. There was one.

He hadn't died alone.

Joy was the hardest thing to bear.

In the weeks following Lasse's death I'd turned down all the well-meaning invitations to dinners and parties, but in mid October I agreed to go to a surprise birthday party for a friend.

And it was fun. I had fun. I laughed a lot, possibly a bit too hysterically. But when the band started playing and the others dragged me on to the dance floor, I couldn't make my body dance along. I stood in the midst of it all, my belly full of life, my legs unmoving, watching the lights dance around the people dancing around me.

Their faces glowed purple and red and green and yellow, and I retreated to a fold-up chair by an empty table, told myself I'd only been pretending to be normal. It felt like I'd fucked Lasse's memory.

Lasse was the first man who really loved me for who I was. All the other guys I met on nights out thought I was too quirky, too silly, too strange, too scantily clad, too childish, too drunk, too high, too much.

But Lasse would lay his forehead against mine. Just think, he'd say, now our brains are only two centimetres of skull apart.

He had a thing for my overbite because it meant he could stick his tongue up under my front teeth, and if my teeth were clenched shut, he'd shift his attention to the body I'd spent my adolescence so ashamed of, kiss the shame away.

Sometimes when we were side by side, he'd take a step back and get me to turn full circle so he could look me up and down, his eyes shining.

Wow! he'd say, pulling me towards him, blushing and giddy with joy, as we tumbled into a heap on his sofa bed.

He sang me love songs, and they were wonderful even though he could barely hit the notes. He drew me when I wasn't looking, absorbed in a trashy magazine with a double chin, or at the hairdresser's with my hair full of foil. As time went by, I adopted his gaze. I'd never felt as comfortable in my own skin as I did when I was with him.

And now, when I looked in the mirror, an ordinary face stared back at me. All that remained: my floppy hair, sticky-out teeth, poor posture, small breasts, inflated pregnancy limbs.

Lasse had taught Elmer to say *Mum is beautiful*, and I wasn't proud of my narcissism when I found myself asking Elmer if I was beautiful and he dutifully replied yes.

Grief is a language of lack. My longing for intimacy tugged relentlessly at my heart, but I had no one to share it with.

I could tell people I missed him.

I could tell my sisters and my girlfriends: *I miss his kiss, I miss his touch.*

But I couldn't seem to get it past my lips that I missed his dick.

The day I found a shrivelled pink penis ring at the back of the top drawer, I wept. I held it in my open palm and sobbed over everything that was ours alone.

Everything that had now turned to ash, his dick included.

I dialled the number of a grief support group in Aarhus. By the time an elderly woman answered, my heart was racing and my armpits were drenched in sweat. Her voice was calm as she introduced herself as the group's secretary.

Hi, I'm Puk. Oh God, I'm crying already. Sorry. I'm sorry. I'm calling because my husband died six weeks ago.

That's not something you should be apologizing for. It sounds like you're having a rough time of it.

I don't know what to do, I can't bear it, it just hurts so much.

The phone was hot on my cheek.

I understand, she said. Maybe you could tell me a bit about yourself and your situation, so I can get to know you a bit better? You sound quite young?

I'm twenty-six, and that's the thing, I don't feel old enough for any of this. None of my friends or family have lost anyone like this. They're trying, but they have no idea what it's like, they're kind, but it doesn't help, that's why I called, I thought maybe there'd be others who have been through something similar, oh and I forgot to say, we have a two-year-old, and our second child is due in December. My husband died of heart failure, it just happened, out of the blue. Sorry, I'm blabbering, I'm just so confused.

That's OK. And you're thinking of joining a support group?

I don't know. Maybe. I thought you might know another single mum my age who also just lost her husband?

She paused.

Oh, I wish I could help, but most of the people in our groups are quite a bit older than you. I'm sure you could still get a lot out of talking to them though.

Thanks. But really I just wanted to talk with another young woman with small children. It's the children I'm worried about most. How I'm going to get them through it.

The woman was quiet for a moment.

There is a woman who joined a while ago, she must be in her early thirties. Her husband was in a car accident about half a year ago, something like that. She has kids too, one of them must still be a baby.

Was she also pregnant when he died?

I sounded so excited.

No, I'm afraid she wasn't . . . Well, you know what I mean. But her youngest is very young. How about I try to get in touch with her for you? Are you still there?

Yes.

My head felt excessively heavy. It hurt my neck to hold it up.

It's just that I'm pregnant. I have no idea how I'm supposed to give birth without my husband there. He'll never get to hold the baby. I'll never even have a photo of them together. If I could just have that . . .

I'm so sorry.

No, I'm sorry, I'm not sure what I was hoping for. I'll think about joining a group, thank you for your time, and for letting me talk to you, I'd better be going now.

I hung up. The phone slid out of my hand and on to the floor.

Elmer and I were in a vast freight yard. It was dark and we were surrounded by abandoned train carriages, their blackened windows like empty eye sockets. Heavy chains hung down from the sky above us, swaying slowly.

I had a torch but the battery was low and it kept flickering out. Something was coming towards us through the dark, that much we knew. Sometimes the torch beam illuminated the backs of three figures, my mum and two of my sisters, but they weren't really there.

We were looking for something.

In the distance I could see a patch of dull silver, bobbing up and down in mid-air. Then it began to grow, moving towards us. Soon the patch was only a couple of metres away.

It was part of a man. He was dressed in the running gear with reflective strips I'd given Lasse for his last birthday. He wore a loose balaclava and a trilby hat on top of it, but you could still see that he didn't have eyebrows or hair. His eyes were vacant, his forehead bluish-white. His windproof jacket was slightly open, rust-coloured freckles on waxlike skin.

The man picked Elmer up and started wrapping him in the chains, then he lifted the balaclava away from his face. He was going to bite him. I lunged forward, clawing at the chains, desperately trying to break Elmer free.

My mum and sisters were standing next to us now, their backs still turned. The man loosened his grip on Elmer and turned to me. He pinned my arms behind my back and held them tight. I couldn't move as he shoved his crotch between my legs and jutted his hairless chin so far forward it almost made contact with mine.

I woke bolt upright in bed, gasping for air. Lasse's duvet was on the floor.

I was sitting on a chair with a clump of red plasticine in my hand, a sickly-sweet smell. The other mothers were chatting around me, lifting cups of coffee to mouths, slurping and setting them back down again, balanced precariously on flattened strips of plasticine.

The kids had left the table and were busy jumping about on the sofa, giggling away.

All except for Elmer, standing alone in the corner of the living room, turning a wooden toy over in his hands.

Couldn't he just play with the others for once, I was thinking, when there was a sudden crash. Two of the kids had fallen from the sofa mid-hug, their faces smashing into each other as they hit the wooden floor. Cue screams and parents leaping up to pull the wailing children into their arms. Their distress caused tears to well up in my own eyes, but I swallowed them back – it wasn't my turn to cry.

Elmer was watching the commotion with a blank expression on his face. Crushing the toy in his hands. Under his breath, in a monotone, he repeated the same words over and over:

Elmer is happy. Elmer is happy. Elmer is happy.

V

Seven weeks into widowhood, I found myself in the home of a woman who designed clothes for children – a semi-detached house in Løgten, just outside of Aarhus. My parents had advised me to resume my internship, get back on the horse and on with life. I'd done as they said.

The designer's house brought up the rear of a row of new-builds with estate cars parked in the driveways. Her drive was empty, her husband had just left for work. Mist hovered over the street. There were dewy spiderwebs draped between the branches of recently planted hedges, child-size football goals and balance bikes strewn across otherwise orderly front lawns.

We sat facing each other in the open-plan kitchen. The woman's daughter had just modelled one of her mum's designs for me and was now curled up on her lap.

I asked the designer how she'd come up with the idea for a different kind of snap fastener on bibs, nodding my approval and diligently writing down the answer in my notebook: her daughter's hair kept getting caught in the fasteners.

As I followed up with a question about the penguin print on her onesies and joggers, I smiled at her daughter, and thought about my own son, whose dad hadn't driven off to work this morning. My son, who was in grief and in nursery on this foggy autumn day, who had split my lip two days ago in one of his tantrums, leaving me sitting perplexed in the nursery cloakroom in front of the other parents whose mouths weren't bleeding and who didn't have a dead spouse and who weren't about to give birth to their second child alone.

And yet here I was in another woman's house in Løgten, betraying Elmer to write an article about snap fasteners or organic cotton. Snap fasteners *and* organic cotton, sorry, I didn't get much sleep last night. The children's clothes designer laughed and I laughed along with her.

On the train home I realized I'd never be happy again.

Then I wished that her husband had died instead of mine.

What had become of me?

I'd been a climbing plant, growing up Lasse, winding myself around him. He'd held me up and I'd flowered, and now I was writhing around on the ground, twisting myself into knots and trying to find my own stem to climb up.

I was Lasse's widow and the boys' mother, that much I knew. Beyond that, I had no idea.

There was the adventurous spirit who, nineteen years old and having just graduated from gymnasium, went off to Thailand with her big sister. She'd wanted to experience the world with her backpack on her back, wash her underwear in sinks and eat noodles standing up on the hot asphalt, to drive around in tuk-tuks and hike through jungle and get blisters and mosquito bites and sunburn and to sit cross-legged on a sandy beach, smoking joints into the sunset.

There was the wild child, the entertainer, forever cracking jokes and persuading unsuspecting taxi drivers to let her take the wheel at 4 a.m., barefoot, with the windows rolled down and her friend laughing her ass off in the back seat, the three of them singing all the way down Amagerbrogade.

And then there was the budding investigative journalist, soon to graduate and launch herself into the world, digging up unlikely truths, bypassing red herrings to write stories that pulled no punches. She was going to crack the establishment wide open, live in New York and land exclusive interviews with famous artists and send her articles home to Danish newspapers, her byline on the front page. She was going to entice, provoke, make her mark on the world.

It seemed almost laughable to try to reconstruct the carefree young woman I'd been. Brown legs and long islands and backpacks and drink-driving and journalist dreams that, in hindsight, might have belonged to others more than they'd ever really belonged to me.

Because there was also the girl who gave it all up in a heartbeat for a boyfriend.

In Thailand I could barely tear my eyes away from the photo of him in my notebook. In all my emails home I wrote that I wished he was here and that I was being careful with money so I'd still be able to pay my half of the deposit on an apartment when I returned, and should I buy an Asian cushion cover and bring it back for us? Eventually my sister gave me a poke in the ribs and said, for God's sake, I was there with her, not him, and anyway it was far too early for decorative cushions. But it was too late, my mind was already racing ahead, was already home in Denmark, building a life with Lasse.

Because above all I'd been the girl, and then the woman, who wanted to start a family. Who, sitting on the toilet four years later with my trousers around my ankles and a positive pregnancy test balanced on my knee, felt surprise and then, a second later, everything falling into place. Felt that right here, on this toilet, life was really about to begin.

I'd never dreamed about a life as a single mum.

I wanted to give Elmer and his little brother a good childhood. But it was impossible to imagine anything ever really being good again.

Lasse and I had made every decision together, from which wellies to buy to who to vote for to how many children to have. Now *Shall we go left or right?* had become *Why would I even go?*

Why would I go anywhere, when every step I took was a step further away from him?

I thought: If Lasse could see me now, would he even like me?

Would he like the way I asked my sister not to speak on the phone to her husband in my presence, because I didn't have my own husband to call?

The way I was only able to feel my love for Elmer *after* I'd put him to bed each night?

Or the way I counted the days between phone calls from friends and family only to conclude that they'd never really been there for me, never really cared about me anyway?

I no longer understood how it was possible for anyone to be as unproblematically happy as I once had been.

The photos from our summer road trip through Europe were just a few months old, but already they told of a reality I doubted had ever really existed. Looking at them felt like an act of violence.

A man sitting on a bench, drawing a church in his sketchbook with a stick of charcoal.

A toddler standing on a street in Prague, in T-shirt, nappy and sandals, watching a tram and holding on to his dad's hand.

A woman wearing a red straw hat, grinning and looking at a man who was grinning and looking at the camera.

People that had ceased to exist.

Lasse's shoes still lined the hall. I couldn't bring myself to move them.

If I slid my hands into them and ran my fingers over the hollows his toes had pressed into the insoles, and if I kept my eyes shut, I could just about rebuild him. A Lasse hologram, flickering inside a pair of solid trainers that were the only thing anchoring him to reality.

In our early twenties, Lasse and I scrimped and saved our student grants so we could spend the summer driving around America. We drove through Death Valley, gazed out into the Grand Canyon, spent a night in Las Vegas and whiled away endless hours on endless highways, side by side in our rental car, listening to country music on the radio as freight trains trundled through the dust along the tracks beside us.

One day we spotted a dust devil in the rear-view mirror. We made a U-turn so we could drive through it, and when a tumble-weed came bouncing across the road, I hopped out of the car and caught it. We'd only ever seen them in cartoons. It travelled with us on the back seat for several weeks.

We ate burgers and drank refill iced tea at diners where the waitresses introduced themselves by name. One of them had dentures and a baby-pink gingham dress that just about came down to her thighs.

After sunset, we'd pull in at cheap motels and make love on threadbare sheets, falling asleep naked in each other's arms as the light from the TV painted the walls of our room a flickering blue.

One night I was jerked awake by the sensation of my body

being lifted up. Seconds later, I found myself on the floor in a tangle of sheets, Lasse sitting dumbfounded beside me. He'd picked me up and leaped out of the bed with me in his arms. We were both shaking.

What were you thinking? I shouted.

I had a long scratch on my arm, little droplets of blood seeping out of it.

He stammered that he'd had a nightmare. He'd dreamed I was tied to the tracks and a freight train was speeding towards me.

He'd thrown himself in front of the train to save me.

I dreamed that Lasse's friends were moving house and I had to help them.

The house had many rooms, all of them piled high with mess. Everything had to be packed away into boxes until each room was empty. I laboured for hours, carrying the boxes in front of my enormous stomach with my arms outstretched. Elmer was there too; he flickered between being himself and being Lasse, sitting in the middle of the chaos, refusing to lift a finger. At some point I'd had enough of his idleness and told him as much. It wasn't on, he ought to be helping out. He said he was tired and just wanted to sleep.

He went into an empty room and I wasn't allowed to follow him like I usually did when I put him to bed. He closed the door on me.

When I sneaked in later to check on him, he'd already fallen asleep. He was lying on a steep stairwell that spiralled down into nothingness.

I sat on the sofa making my way through the stack of letters that had been piling up all week. My stomach was now so big I could balance them on it. My feet were tucked under Elmer's duvet – as was Elmer, snuggled up next to me, engrossed in yet another cartoon.

One of the letters was from Lasse's insurance company.

By now I'd grown so weary of these official-looking envelopes with their little plastic windows. They always wanted me to log in somewhere with a code, fill out forms and send in documentation. I took little care as I ripped the envelope open.

It said I was rich.

It said Lasse had taken out a life insurance policy to provide for me and the children.

I brought the piece of paper right up to my nose, blinking in disbelief at the number printed in bold. The value of Lasse, double-underlined.

This is what he was worth. Here is the compensation for your grief.

Stubborn man. I'd always made it clear to him what I thought of life insurance, accident insurance and the like: all a bit hysterical, irrelevant. Because if either of us were ever to seriously injure ourselves, I'd reasoned, money would be the last of our problems.

I gaped out into the room.

Would I change my mind now? Start splashing about in Lasse's death money?

I was used to not having very much money. A childhood of shared bedrooms and second-hand clothes and four siblings and a mum who cried the one time my dad bought a jar of acacia honey for thirty kroner without asking her first.

My parents had worked hard to make ends meet, but they also seemed to get a bit of a thrill out of throwing the unpaid bills up in the air, herding us all into the car and driving to France for the holidays, only to return weeks later and tear their hair out all over again.

Meanwhile, Lasse had grown up with parents who'd never dream of spending more than they had. They opened presents without tearing the paper so they could fold it up again for next year; they mended socks, built their own garage, tiled their own bathroom and took care of their bikes and cars like they were priceless works of art.

That was the foundation Lasse and I had built our own lives on. We did our best to get by and wasted as little as possible.

My mouth felt dry. I ran my tongue slowly over my front teeth as I looked down at the sofa. One of the seams on the arm-rest had come undone, the cover was discoloured. I could buy a new one.

I folded the letter up and slid it back into the envelope. In one fell swoop, my financial problems had been rendered obsolete. Manic laughter burst out from the TV.

Then came the Sunday when I lost track of the Sundays.

My so-far weekly marker of how much time had passed since I'd last seen Lasse alive: a painful milestone that doubled as a reminder that, in spite of everything, we were still going.

At first I thought myself sloppy, but I soon came to see my forgetfulness as evidence of progress. I'd now moved so far away from him that it no longer made sense to account for the loss in weeks.

I rarely cried in front of others any more. My skin had thickened, developing resistance against all the trigger words that had previously thrown me into despair.

Heart. Dad. Run. Architect. Death. Dream. Ambulance. Look forward to. Birth. Bee. Cardiac unit. Carbonara. Man. New York. Marathon. Half-marathon. Umbilical cord. Parents. Porridge. Defibrillator. Kiss. Family.

I'd grown accustomed to being a canvas upon which other people painted their own versions of me.

You're such a strong woman, they'd say, or: *You're coping so incredibly well.*

Apparently, everyone I knew had become overnight experts

in human strength, since they all seemed to identify it so easily in me. Many offered up their own tales of grief by way of consolation. Like we were in the same club.

People who haven't lost someone themselves simply aren't able to relate to what you're going through, said a peripheral acquaintance.

She'd lost her own husband a year ago, aged fifty. She knew what grief felt like. Not to compare, she added, having just done exactly that.

The losses and predicaments of others were nothing compared to mine, and even though I shook my head dismissively whenever they called me *strong*, *tough*, *superwoman*, eventually I felt those adjectives begin to harden in me.

Because they were right. I was coping with the uncopeable.

I took care of a toddler, completed my internship, made conversation by the coffee machine. My mascara was impeccable, our home tidy. I was polite and volunteered wise words about life and death and Lasse and even remembered to ask others how they were doing. I kept his grave fresh with flowers and dabbed the appropriate quantity of tears from the corners of my eyes. My pregnancy was beautiful, my grief was healthy, I had regular appointments with a psychologist and spoke openly about all of it, progressing through the various stages of grief slightly faster than I was supposed to.

I played the role of the strong widow to perfection. If grief was a competition, I was going for gold.

And then there was Elmer, who completely failed to play the role of cute, grieving child.

He never cried for his loss, but he screamed at everything else, hitting and biting the other children at nursery.

Whenever he slapped me in the face, I'd gently remind him that I didn't like it when he did that, that what I really liked was being stroked, and when he gave me another slap, I told him calmly and firmly that he wasn't allowed to do that, while my own palm itched to do the same.

He no longer wanted to wave goodnight to the star. When I dragged him out on to the balcony, he ran straight back into the living room and left me standing alone in the dark.

I tried to tell myself that it was just a phase, a phase we simply had to get through, that I should try to enjoy the last few weeks I had with him before the baby was born. But it still felt like an enormous relief when 7 p.m. came around and I could finally put him to bed. An end to the fights, screams and futility, another evening of numbing myself on the sofa with Channel 4 and TV3.

One night I woke around midnight to the sound of Elmer talking to himself in his room in a little croaky voice. I tiptoed over the rug in the hall, held my breath and tried to make out the mumbled words.

Dad runs away, he said hesitantly, then let out a frustrated sigh before breaking into heart-wrenching sobs.

I opened the door and when he saw me, he shouted:

No! Not Mum!

Still, his arms reached out for me as I went to him, and for once he didn't mind being carried into the double bed to sleep by my side.

His skin was warm under his onesie and he smelled of duvet and the not entirely unpleasant odour of nappy. It hurt to hear him crying, but I also liked lying there next to him in the darkness. It was the first time in a long time that I hadn't felt like a bad mother.

As he settled down, he repeated the words he'd said before.

Dad runs up, up, up into the sky. Up on to a star.

He pointed up and out, through the curtains, to where the stars hung in the vastness of the night.

Dad runs up the stairs? he asked. And it finally dawned on

me: my story about the star was incomplete. Because, even for a two-year-old, it didn't make sense that you could run up and on to something that hung in the empty vacuum of the sky.

Yes, Elmer! He ran up the star stairs. You can't see them in the dark, but they're there. There's a big, long staircase all the way up to Dad's star. It's a very special kind of staircase that disappears when you want to go down it again.

He let me stroke his hair. He was breathing calmly now. The pale light from outside cut through the gap between the curtains and landed on the duvet like a lumpy moon landscape.

We lay for a long time in silence.

Will Mum run up the star stairs too? he asked.

I promised him the impossible.

Elmer and I were sitting in the back of Helle's car on the E45 from Southern Jutland to Aarhus. It was afternoon. Helle had offered to drive us home after a weekend at my parents' place, and now I sat gazing out at the landscape of stubble fields and deserted farmhouses shrouded in a feeble fog.

A pair of crows caught my eye, their black legs perched on the hard shoulder, pecking away at something furry that seemed to be stuck to the asphalt. As we drove past, one of them snapped at the other viciously with its beak.

P4 streamed out of the speakers as cars sped past us in the express lane. Elmer dozed in the child seat next to me.

We had just passed Ejer Bavnehøj when Helle's phone started ringing from her bag on the passenger seat.

Keeping her eyes trained on the road and one hand on the steering wheel, she reached into her bag and rummaged around with the other, found her phone and answered the call with a quick *one second*. Then she indicated and drove the car over on to the hard shoulder, braked and switched on the hazard lights.

I watched the cars zipping by, shaking Helle's car as they passed.

What's going on? I asked, but she already had the phone to her ear.

She said yes twice, then handed the phone to me.

It was a magazine journalist. He was quick to offer his condolences, said he'd tried to call me on my own phone several times and had left a message on my answering machine, but maybe he'd got the wrong number?

He hadn't. No, sorry, I didn't want to tell my story to his readers.

And I respect that of course, I really do, he said. But I've often heard others say that it can be very therapeutic to get it out, inspire others with it. It sounds like you're an incredibly strong woman.

Again I said no, and goodbye.

I gave Helle her phone and she put it back into her bag. I turned and looked anxiously out of the back window as she pulled out on to the motorway again. First gear, all clear. Second gear, cars appearing over the ridge behind us. Third gear, they pulled over into the express lane. Fourth gear, the motorway began to hiss beneath us. Fifth gear.

I looked at Helle behind the wheel, her eyes fixed on the road. I looked at the sleeping boy by my side and laid a hand on my stomach. Then I caught sight of myself in the rear-view mirror. My eyes were glazed over and hollow in my pale face.

On Lasse's deathbed I promised I'd tell his sons about him every single day. I'd show them his sketchbooks, tell them tales of their one and only, loving, thoughtful architect of a father until they couldn't help but fall in love with him too.

Another promise I couldn't keep.

For a long time I weighed up every one of my decisions based on what Lasse would have thought of them. In BabySam I deliberated over nursing pillows, unable to decide whether Lasse would have preferred blue cows or green horses.

Sometimes I had to push him violently aside in order to function at all, tripping over his trainers in the hall and deciding not to care what he thought of my new haircut.

Every time I relegated him to the shadows of my consciousness, there was an equally powerful force trying to pull him back out into the light again. It broke my heart to see him skulking off to a dark corner of the living room while I read Elmer a bedtime story instead of going out on to the balcony and waving to the star.

We'd never managed to agree on a name for the baby. We'd narrowed it down to two – I preferred one and Lasse the other. Now, either way, it would be my decision, and somehow that felt like an infringement on Lasse's parenthood.

At the funeral, someone had said that of course the baby should be named after Lasse. But Lasse was the name of my lover, now my loss, my longing. I didn't want the baby to have that kind of start in life. And besides, he was *my* child too.

That was my first, tentative, protest against Lasse.

Shadow Dad protested back. First I'd feel his incriminating gaze, then his voice in my head.

Do you really think you can get away with choosing your own favourite name for our child? he asked.

And once he'd broken the silence, the questions escalated.

Are you taking advantage of the situation to force your own agenda? Are you going to give them the chance to grow up as our children or just yours? Admit it, weren't you a little bit happy when you got the money? Or have you been so busy playing the victim that you forgot to thank me?

It was maddening. We started fighting in the evenings, whispering so as not to wake Elmer.

Easy enough for you to say, I hissed back, why don't you try taking my place for, like, one day? See how it feels to miss *me*. Must be a breeze hovering about up there, hard to go wrong when you're a treasured memory. How about you let *me* disappear for a bit and you can stand here whispering into thin air? And while you're at it, try not sleeping and being heavily pregnant and taking care of a two-year-old. You can even explain to Elmer why you never came home, tell him what actually happened, because I'll be damned if I know, *you're* the one who disappeared, not me.

Lasse became a work of art.

He never lied, said Helle to the priest before the funeral, and the entire family nodded their agreement.

But Lasse lied just as much as the next person.

My love for him was equally matched by my resentment of him; our relationship had been life-affirming and it had also, from time to time, been suffocating.

I loved the father he'd eventually become for Elmer, but that process had been no walk in the park for either of us. For the first three months Elmer had colic and screamed for hours on end. Neither of us had known what to do and we'd taken our powerlessness out on each other.

Lasse thought I should be doing all the shopping and washing-up, seeing as I was at home all day with the baby anyway.

I thought he should be home when he said he would be and not ten minutes later.

He thought I should let him play computer games in the evening once Elmer had settled down.

I thought he should come to bed early with me, so he'd be able to get up in the morning and help out instead of lying around snoozing.

He said it wasn't hard for him to have a child, it was me as a mother he couldn't stand.

I said that was easy enough for him to say, when he didn't contribute to anything to do with our child.

Two days before his final architecture exam, I came down with a throat infection. Hot with fever and with Elmer in tow in the pushchair, I got on the wrong bus to the otolaryngologist, whose office was in a shopping centre outside the city, and when I finally arrived, I could barely speak with my gravel voice.

I sat breastfeeding Elmer while the doctor examined me. She said that the throat infection had evolved into an abscess and I was to go on penicillin right away, and that the penicillin might infiltrate my breast milk.

I called Lasse in tears and asked him to come home so he could look after Elmer – and me – but he said he couldn't. He said I'd have to ask someone else.

A couple of weeks later, when Lasse got up onstage to a shower of awards and grants for his final project, I stood at the back of the room unable to clap because both my arms were holding Elmer, and I felt a pang of resentment. We were the ones he ought to have been gazing down adoringly at from his pedestal.

He got a job at an architectural firm while my own career was being swallowed up by maternity leave before it had really got started. I still dreamed of becoming a journalist, but I wasn't able to separate myself from our child in the way Lasse could.

Lasse was an artist. When he disappeared into his projects or fixated on his dreams, the rest of the world was lost to him.

That glazed look he got, the way he saw right through me

when he was busy building skyscrapers in his head. Or the way he stared out of the window, lost in thought, while Elmer squirmed on the changing table below him, trying to catch his dad's eye.

His persistence and attention to detail made him an exceptional architect: he never compromised, never gave up. But it was this same persistence that pushed him to extremes. It wasn't inconceivable that his body had warned him at some point in the marathon and he'd just kept running, powering through.

Lasse was fallible like everyone else. Like I was too. I didn't love all of his shortcomings; he didn't love all of mine. But they were there.

Routine became my survival strategy. Every day at 3.30 p.m. I'd cycle from my internship to pick Elmer up at nursery. We'd get home, eat cheese and crackers in the kitchen, play for a bit, then I'd put him in front of the TV while I made dinner, which I served at 5.30 p.m. on the dot.

At 6.30 p.m., Elmer would get a bubble bath and afterwards I'd put his pyjamas on, read him a bedtime story on the sofa, then carry him to his cot, sing him a goodnight song, switch the main light off and the fairy lights around the elephant poster on, tell him I loved him and, at 7 p.m., shut his bedroom door behind me.

Then I'd tidy the kitchen and living room, throw myself on to the sofa and write my diary, the TV chattering away in the background. If Elmer happened to call for me at the wrong moment, I'd start to feel nauseous.

Most nights I had a friend visiting too. Esben had drawn up a rota so there was always someone to keep me company. They would arrive after Elmer was in bed, and sometimes we spoke, but most of the time they just sat next to me on the sofa. At first they had come earlier and made dinner, but they put sweetcorn in the bolognese, used too many pans and spent far too long cooking. The conversations with them as we ate – and as Elmer complained – drove me mad.

If they put things away in the kitchen, it could spark a panic attack the following evening when I couldn't find the trivet, and so couldn't put the pot of soup on the dining table; I had to spoon out portions in the kitchen instead, and while I was busy doing that Elmer might knock a potted plant off the windowsill in the living room, and then I'd have to spend time sweeping up the soil, which meant skipping a couple of pages of the bedtime story so I could still get him to bed by 7 p.m.

When my internship ended, my body was heaving with pain and I was ready to drop, but the thought of going on maternity leave before there was an actual baby to take care of petrified me. Nothing to do, nothing to prove, so much empty time to think again.

I didn't dare to be alone with myself. I began going to the library to get a head start on studying for my next exam, or spent hours trawling through newspapers and Facebook – all in a day's work. I left the library at 3.30 p.m., carried on as before.

One afternoon I'd arranged for Esben, Hans and Helle to pick Elmer up from nursery. They returned to the apartment armed with shopping bags from the market. I gave them a despairing look, but they promised to clean up after themselves.

Elmer's face lit up as they spread the kitchen worktop with apples, oranges, beetroots, carrots and pineapples.

Juicing was one of Lasse's *things*. He'd loved making juice with Elmer. The two of them would stand side by side in the kitchen, Elmer on a stool, Lasse handing him a chunk of apple, which Elmer would drop down the tube, then they'd bend their knees in unison as they watched the fruit get zapped through with a little *pfffzt* sound, the juice flowing out of the machine and into the plastic jug.

When Esben and my parents-in-law started setting up the blender exactly like Lasse used to, I excused myself from the kitchen. It was too much. I wanted to scream that I didn't have the strength for more projects, more *bring Lasse back* projects, but I just sat on the sofa and tried my best to block out the drone and gurgle of the machine.

I took a book from the shelf but couldn't focus on the words, slammed it shut again. I pressed my tongue into the roof of my mouth, tried to breathe calmly.

Eventually Esben came into the living room, carrying a full jug of juice, and set it on the dining table. Elmer tottered in after him and clambered up on to his highchair. His uncle went back into the kitchen for glasses and, just as I managed to form the thought *this won't end well*, Elmer stood up on his chair, grabbed the jug with both hands and tipped two litres of purple juice all over Lasse's handmade dining table. Esben and Helle tried to scrape the pool back into the jug with their hands, spilling more of it on to the floor, where it splashed the chair legs too. I squeezed my eyes shut.

My hair started falling out, and what was left stood up from my scalp like little antennae. I couldn't stop sucking my tongue and the habit was starting to wear away at the roof of my mouth, the strain on my jaw enflaming my headaches.

It was hard to pinpoint what came first, the stress or the fatigue.

I was suffering from serious dyssomnia. The prospect of nightmares put me off falling asleep, so I just lay in the dark, blinking away. And when sleep finally came for me, the baby would wake up, kicking and rolling inside me.

The additional weight and immobility of pregnancy made even something as simple as finding a comfortable sleeping position an enormous undertaking. I propped my stomach up with a duvet and wedged pillows between my knees, but then I'd start thinking about how the duvet I'd rolled into a sausage was Lasse's, and then I'd start thinking about why he no longer needed a duvet, and then I'd lie awake crying and watching the clock on my phone ticking closer and closer to 6 a.m., when Elmer would wake up again.

The letter arrived mid November, *Skejby Hospital* stamped on the envelope. It was from the Cardiology Department, inviting me to a meeting. They'd analysed the test results from Lasse's autopsy, and now they were able to tell us why a young, fit and apparently healthy man could suffer sudden heart failure, why cardiac massage and all the other resuscitation attempts had failed.

My fear that the children might have inherited whatever Lasse died of was so crippling that I hadn't told a soul about it. I'd barely even let myself think it.

With my heart in my throat, I waited in the corridor with my in-laws. I clutched the envelope in my hand and declined Hans's offers of coffee. He came back with a glass of apple juice for me instead.

A doctor arrived and invited us to follow him. He showed us into a room and barely gave us a chance to get seated before launching in.

It's good news, in light of everything, he said. Lasse didn't suffer from a hereditary condition.

Åh!

Relief flooded my body. Helle tried to take my hand but I snapped it away.

When we conducted the autopsy, the doctor continued, we were puzzled by how big Lasse's heart was. So we took a closer look and we could see that it was full of scar tissue from a previous inflammation. It's called myocarditis.

It was the first time I'd heard any of these words, but I did my best to catch them and hold on tight. Knew I'd soon find myself repeating them to anyone and everyone who asked.

Death had a name.

Myocarditis.

It was a twisted kind of comfort to learn that Lasse had been terminally ill.

I swallowed *previous inflammation* as if it was something all hearts had, mulling over the words as my medically well-versed in-laws nodded their understanding and asked specific questions.

Could you tell from the tissue when the scars were formed? Lasse's sister asked, and the doctor shook his head.

It's impossible to tell. They could date back to childhood, or sometime later. We have no way of knowing. What we do know is that he was very, very ill at some point in his life. Whenever it was, he got through it then, but after that his heart was in such poor condition, it was unable to withstand excessive strain of any kind. Did he ever complain of chest pain or fatigue?

We looked at each other.

Did he?

I pictured his big, red heart covered in little blotches of infection. The same heart I'd rested my head against night after night.

No. I mean, I don't think so. Sometimes he seemed pretty tired, but that was when he'd been working really hard, I said, thinking of Lasse lying on the floor, his eyes closed and his arms crossed over his chest, instead of playing with Elmer. How pissed off I'd been.

Could that have been his heart? Had I been too hard on him about doing his fair share?

Helle seemed to be thinking along the same lines, retreating into herself, replaying everything back. Then, cautiously, she said:

Once when we were on holiday and Lasse was very young – he must have been eight or something – he came down with a very high fever for a while. We found a tick on him, and as soon as we removed it, the fever went away and he seemed fine again; we just put iodine on it. Do you think it could have been that?

The doctor hesitated.

Possibly, he said, but it's hard to say. It could be anything. It could also be a hefty bout of the flu that just so happened to attach itself to his heart. But seeing as he didn't notice anything until . . .

The doctor put down his papers, laid his arms on the table.

The thing is, myocarditis is the kind of condition you don't know you have until you die of it, he said.

We sat motionless, letting the words sink in.

The doctor asked me if I'd like a copy of the autopsy report. I declined.

Knew I'd never read it. I already understood everything I'd ever come to understand. This was a full stop.

Out in the corridor, Christian suggested we all go down to the hospital canteen for some cake and coffee. A little celebration in spite of everything.

On our way, we passed a young couple holding a newborn baby. They looked tired and happy, cocooned in the unmistakable glow of new parenthood. She was wearing sweatpants and walking with careful little post-partum steps; he carried the sleeping baby with exaggerated tenderness. When he saw us looking, he grinned.

Look, Puk, a little baby! said Hans with a smile.

Yeah, in the arms of his dad! I replied, tears already welling up.

The colour drained from Hans's face.

I observed the effect I had on others, how I made them shrivel up, recoil. Then I strode on ahead.

The kind of condition you don't know you have until you die of it.

The following evening I lay on the sofa with my hands on my stomach as the baby made it dance. The past was the past, it no longer applied. I was getting used to how things were, and the baby was about to shake things up all over again.

I tried to make my voice reassuring as I spoke to it:

You are me and I am you. You are him and you are ours. Soon you'll be you, I'll be me, you'll be two, you'll be mine and we'll be us.

I dreamed I had sex with a stranger. I'd gone out intending to score and ended up taking a guy home. He was boring, unattractive and married to another woman.

When I kissed him, I kept my eyes open because I refused to let myself forget that I was cheating. The man's hair reminded me of Lasse's — all blonde and bristly — which only made me more afraid of mixing them up. I didn't know what I was doing. I tried to play horny, sexy, but all I felt was shame.

It was in grief that I really got to know my father-in-law. I'd struggled to understand him before. He seemed to devote his life to things that, to my mind, were utterly trivial: vacuuming cars, putting up fences, repairing toys, cleaning out gutters, feeding chickens, cutting grass, pruning trees and, when the day was done, nodding off in front of the TV with a newspaper or a car magazine in his lap.

I'd always thought his routines tedious and his meticulousness unnecessary, but in the wake of Lasse's death they struck me as kind of beautiful – the satisfaction he drew from a finally completed wooden deck behind the conservatory, his family sitting on it, soaking up the sun and eating his wife's homemade cake as the kids played in the nest swing he'd rigged up between two trees.

He never cried in front of the rest of us, but excused himself quietly if we overdid it. Then I'd spot him down by the kale patch at the end of the garden. I figured he must take his son with him like a little ball of light in his chest – one he could more easily commune with when the two of them were alone.

His grief coexisted with my own, far away but nearby.

We'd lost the same person, but we hadn't suffered the same loss.

Helle, meanwhile, wanted grief to be a shared project. She pulled me into her embrace and told me how much she loved me and the children. But I couldn't return her love, couldn't alleviate her loss, couldn't hold her together when I was still so busy falling to pieces myself.

She showed me drawings from Lasse's childhood and gave me his hand-me-downs for Elmer. But my connection to Lasse's childhood was non-existent; I didn't miss the child, I missed the man.

The shiver that went through my spine when she presented me with Lasse's electric Buzz Lightyear toothbrush. She'd disinfected it with boiling water and thought I could give it to Elmer and say it was a present from Dad.

I threw it in the bin.

When she cried, nobody dared intervene. Even if Lasse's name had come up as part of a funny anecdote, the corners of her mouth would droop, her head would sink to one of her shoulders and her voice would rise to a little squeak. She wanted us to cry together, not laugh, and it was too much for me. In time, I stopped mentioning him in front of her unless it was absolutely necessary.

We were fighting an unspoken fight over Lasse. Who would emerge triumphant, wife or mother?

He was my husband and the father of my children. He was her son.

He was mine. He was hers. But he was never ours.

One month before the due date, my little sister Emma moved in.

I was beginning to go out of my mind with all the people traipsing in and out of my door in shifts, the shrilling doorbell, the wet footprints in the hall, the weekend trips to visit my parents.

Emma showed up with a suitcase full of calm.

She'd just graduated from gymnasium and had been working towards a trip to Uganda. She postponed it and moved on to a mattress on Elmer's bedroom floor.

Of my four siblings, I'd always felt furthest from Emma. She was seven years younger – too far apart to play or party together, but not far apart enough for me to have collected her from nursery or changed her nappy, as I'd done with my brother. To me, Emma was the quiet sister on the back seat, the timid figure hovering at the edge of our holiday photos.

I cleared a couple of shelves in Elmer's cupboard for her clothes.

She never knew what to say when I cried or had panic attacks or claimed there was nothing more to live for and anyway what was the point. She was just there. Often, she cried too.

She understood instinctively that I couldn't tolerate touch, and she didn't try to pet me the way I hated others doing – to the extent that I'd started sitting in the armchair if my guests sat in the middle of the sofa. With Emma, it wasn't a problem. She listened to me with a little furrow in her brow, and when I was done speaking, she looked away.

She went out for snacks, put up with my manic housekeeping rules and sat with me in the evenings watching *The Family from Bryggen* and *The Young Mothers*. She read Elmer goodnight stories, dropped him off and picked him up from nursery, all without threatening my maternal role. In the mornings, her glasses lay next to mine in the bathroom.

When my contractions started one afternoon in early December, she sat beside me and timed each interval.

VI

Streets sailing by, white frost-flowers climbing up the darkened windows, and the taxi driver rolling them down every time I had a contraction so the wind bit and blew at the topmost strands of my damp hair.

The contractions had begun the previous day, and I'd since spent hours sitting in the shower, propped up by a stool, hot water raining down on to my lower back. I was too exhausted to tell the driver that every gust of air felt like an icy whiplash.

On the back seat: Emma, Helene, Kira.

They'd put my suitcase in the boot. A change of clothes, a pile of maternity pads, winter coat and a velour babygrow – brown with white spots – as well as my diary and a photo of Lasse I still hadn't got around to framing.

In the delivery room, a birthing pool had been filled for me. Sinking down into the warm water was an elixir for my pain. The radio was playing on low.

We discussed intervals, dilation, mucus plugs, breathing, membrane rupture. On the whiteboard, the midwife had written: *Puk and friends Helene, Kira and Emma. Expecting her second child.*

No mention of Lasse.

He was hovering there the whole time, but at a distance. I didn't pay him any attention. This was no place for grief.

I was all body.

My stomach stuck out of the pool and Emma ladled warm water over it. Helene plied me with fruit juice and pressed a damp flannel to my forehead. My hand reached out for Kira's and she grabbed it and held on tight.

Sloshing water, soft music, neither joy nor grief, past nor future, just the oscillating sensation of body, at once submerged in an ocean of warmth and about to implode.

One song came to an end and another started playing: a chord, then a voice that brought me out of my body and into emotion. *Sometimes I feel like throwing my hands up in the air –*

At our wedding, Helene and two other friends had worn purple dresses and performed Florence + the Machine's 'You've Got the Love', guitars and all. I'd been sitting on Lasse's lap, my arms wrapped around his neck. Now the song filled the delivery room.

A contraction rippled through me. I lost control of my breathing and my pelvic bones crunched like a walnut in a nutcracker as the memories came rolling in.

Our wedding turned to Elmer's birth. Lasse holding my hand and counting up to ten and down from ten for every contraction. Kira's hands with her painted nails became Lasse's rectangular hands. The same hands that had clumsily strapped a tiny nappy on to Elmer under the heat lamp in the first hour of his life.

It was too much. He'd betrayed me. I wasn't supposed to be lying here alone. The pain was insane.

Turn it off! I begged.

Either be here for me or stay the fuck away. What was I think-ing? He had to go. Florence was silenced, the contraction waned, and I sent Lasse out of the room.

I got my breathing back under control just in time for my abdomen to contract again, the mind-shattering pain pierced only by a mammalian roar – mine.

Then I pushed.

His head came out in a torrent of blood. We were face to face.

It's a stargazer, cried the midwife in wonder.

I caught a brief glimpse of his mouth opening and closing underwater before I summoned the last dregs of my strength, propelled myself through the flames and felt the rest of his body slip out and away, and then there he was, the whole of him, at the bottom of the pool. He made a little attempt to swim; his head collided with my ankle and it felt warm and smooth. I gasped.

The midwife lifted him out of the water and placed him on my chest, and he pushed his hands against it and raised his heavy head, blinking the water away and gazing up at me with big round eyes.

Wow! we said to each other.

There you were.

My senses burst wide open: the warmth of his skin, the soft purple nails, the tadpole-like body, his shoulder blades rising and falling in small, jerky movements, the wet hair-fluff and the howl that came from him and travelled out into every corner of the world.

Never before had I felt so elated. Never before had I felt so bereft.

I let my head fall back on to the edge of the pool and sobbed up into the sky.

Can you see him, Lasse? Can you see how beautiful our son is?

Thank you, I said, over and over, as all the women around us started to cry. Professionals no longer professional, friends no longer steadfast pillars of support, we gave ourselves over to feeling, we sobbed and laughed and stroked and watched and moaned and sighed until it was time to get my newborn son out of the ruby-red water.

Someone put a little knitted hat on his head, and the midwife passed Emma the scissors.

I'd already decided she would be the one to cut the cord, she would be the one he'd bond with. She wiped her eyes on her shirt, then cut.

Who'll hold him while Mum gets out of the pool? the midwife asked.

I nodded at Emma again, but she shook her head reluctantly, clearly not wanting to be responsible for an accident with a newborn baby who'd already lost his dad. I insisted.

She took the swaddle of baby in her arms and held on to him as if he were a porcelain vase while I crawled cautiously out of the pool, blood running down my inner thighs. The midwife wiped it away, pressed a towel to my crotch. I hobbled over to the bed and pulled myself up on to it.

The room was snug and softly lit, the heat lamp already switched on above the table where my son was about to be weighed and measured.

I reached out to Emma so I could take over. The ten steps I'd already walked away from him were ten steps too far. One tiny paw ventured out of the towel, then his fingers spread with an abrupt movement and closed around my index finger. His forehead wrinkled in concentration and his mouth began to peck its way over my ribcage until he found a nipple to attach himself to.

I was surrounded by people and utterly alone.

Do you think he looks like a Kaj too? I thought. I tried to imagine Lasse's reaction.

He was still sucking, his gaze never leaving mine.

Hi there, Kaj, I murmured.

He had Lasse's eyes, I knew Lasse would be proud of that, and I felt a lump forming in my throat.

The life they could have had together.

I bit my lip. I couldn't start shaking again: the midwife was still sewing me up.

Kaj closed his eyes, woozy with raw milk and exhaustion. I asked for my phone and called Helle. There was no one else in the world who so wanted to make the connection between the loss of Lasse and the birth of our baby. Normally I refused her sentimentality, but not this time.

He's here, I told her. He's sleeping now, but when he looked at me, it was just like looking into Lasse's eyes.

I was whispering.

Åh.

She was too.

I can hear his little squeaks, she said.

I told her his weight and measurements, and a bit about the midwife and how it had all gone.

He came out a stargazer, Helle, isn't that beautiful? As if he turned to face his dad.

Pumped full of emotion and hormones as I was, for once, Helle and I were on exactly the same wavelength.

The life they could have had together.

I was allowed to stay on at the postnatal ward for a few days to prepare for life as a single mum of two. Emma went back to the apartment to look after Elmer.

Before the birth, my arms had been in a perpetual state of tension, boxing gloves on, ready to do battle. Now they hung limp and useless at my sides.

When Elmer came to visit, I almost didn't recognize him in the waterproof trousers he'd borrowed from nursery. It was like I could only be a mum for one child at a time. I was sitting on the sofa with my parents, breastfeeding Kaj, and I wanted nothing more than to pull Elmer into me. He stood there looking awkwardly around the room as Emma helped him out of his boots.

Do you want to have a go holding your brother, Elmer? I asked.

He did, and he crawled up next to me and held out his arms.

Kaj was bundled up in a cone of duvets. I detached him from my breast and laid him gently down in Elmer's lap, holding my breath as I positioned Elmer's elbow under Kaj's neck through the duvet.

One brother looked down at the other without a word. Then Elmer moved his face closer to Kaj's and we all smiled, relieved by his curiosity. We were hurrying to whip out our phones when Elmer suddenly lurched down and dealt Kaj a well-aimed headbutt.

We all threw ourselves at him simultaneously, but Elmer had already pushed his brother away with both hands. I only just managed to catch Kaj as he fell.

No! You can't do that! I shouted, shocked. Elmer looked around in surprise.

Someone had given us Mats Letén's *Kaj* books as a gift, and I pulled Elmer on to my lap so I could read them to him.

Kaj is missing. Where is Kaj?

But the story was quickly over and he didn't want to hear it again.

I asked Emma to stay in the room with Kaj so Elmer and I could have some alone time. I took his hand and led him to the family room, where there was a play kitchen and a few boxes of toys. We stood uncertainly in front of them. I couldn't for the life of me remember what he liked to play with.

Shall we build a train track? I asked, kneeling down on the floor and reaching for the pieces, but he just turned back towards one of the boxes and swept his hand indifferently over its contents.

Then he went over to the toy kitchen and tentatively opened the oven. I crawled after him. My stitches were sweating, my maternity pad felt wet.

Mmm! Will you also make some dinner for me? I said, handing him a plastic chicken thigh. How about you fry this up for me?

He took it and put it down on the stove, then walked back to the door, waiting to leave.

By then, I'd grown used to lying in bed talking to Shadow Dad. Sometimes we fought, but most of the time he stayed silent as I showered him with adoring monologues. I wished him goodnight and told him a bit about my day and Elmer's achievements. I said I loved him.

I was convinced my words were heard. I could sense him with me, a presence to latch on to whenever I shut my eyes. He existed at the edge of the darkness under my eyelids like a little glint of light, and the light was his love, still going strong.

At the hospital he was no longer there.

My room was dark apart from the strip of light coming under the door. I lay in bed and spoke to Lasse, but now it felt contrived, fake.

I got out of bed, picked up a sleeping Kaj and went over to the window, opened the blind. We stood facing the frozen night, watching the wind blow in circles around the reddish glow of the street lights, the chill whitening the glass and making the hair on my arms stand up.

You're a dad again, Lasse.

The stars shone in the sky, mocking me.

I didn't cry. I was waiting for an answer. I held Kaj up to the heavens.

Do you see him? Do you *see* him?

The only sound came from the gust of wind against the window. I took a step back and hugged Kaj close to me.

I'd loved the stargazer metaphor. But the reality of giving birth to a stargazer is that the baby exits the womb with the widest part of its head pressing down against the pelvis, meaning the birth takes longer and generally results in a lot of extra post-natal discomfort.

For me it meant a burst perineum and getting stitched up in several places. For Kaj it meant a crick in his neck for the first few months of his life, which also meant relentless, colic-like crying.

Every trip to the toilet was an ordeal, every shit that squeezed its way out of my arsehole seemed to tear my stitches apart. I would sit there, red-faced and sweating, my hands pressing the tiles on either side of me, gasping in pain. And as the shit finally lumped its way out of me and into the bloody toilet bowl, I pictured the skin of a bongo drum being stretched taut by string.

I began to feel a deep resentment of Lasse's wretched star, and all it stood for, simmering inside me.

How could I be so unhappy when Kaj had just come into the world? How could I be so happy when Lasse had just left it?

The day Kaj and I were discharged from the ward, there was a Christmas party at Elmer's nursery. The plan had been to swing by the apartment, drop off the suitcase and change from sweatpants into a shirt dress that would conceal my postnatal stomach. But then Kaj wanted milk, and then he shat his nappy, then he wanted more milk.

By the time I'd wrapped him in the sling and jogged down the stairs, I was already running far too late. It took me half the street to realize I'd forgotten the changing supplies. Back up in the apartment, everything swimming before my eyes, I threw a handful of nappies and a pack of wet wipes into a plastic bag, then hurried back out again, hobbling along the icy pavement as fast as I could with a baby on my stomach and stitches between my legs. When I finally made it to the nursery cloakroom, it was full of boots and noise. They'd already danced around the tree outside and now they were taking their outdoor clothes off.

The other parents were helping their kids. I looked around until I spotted Elmer sitting on the lap of one of the nursery staff, who was unzipping his snowsuit.

I was out of breath, and I couldn't even sit down next to him because of the sling.

Hey you, did you have fun dancing around the Christmas tree? Sorry Mum came so late, Kaj needed milk.

I ran my fingers through Elmer's hair, staticky from his hat. There was a thick smell of æbleskiver in the air and the hubbub in the room drilled into my skull.

Did Father Christmas come?

Yeah!

He stood up and started to show me what was in his goodie bag when one of the other mums put a hand on my back. I flinched and turned my head a bit too fast, a little shooting pain in my neck.

You just gave birth? Congratulations! Let's have a look at the little prince.

She dipped her head towards my throat and pulled the sling a bit to one side. Her cheek smelled of ice and a transparent droplet of snot was working its way out of her nostril.

Kaj stirred; his mouth searched my shirt, found a button, went back to searching.

Please, Mum, can I have some mooore – she made her voice bright and babyish, then cooed:

Åh, isn't he beautiful!

Thanks, I said, bouncing my legs to send him back to sleep. The pain in my neck travelled up to behind one of my eyeballs.

Elmer tugged at my coat.

You forget how small they are, it's incredible, and to think that Otto was so small only two years ago, time really does fly, doesn't it. How did the birth go? And how's it going with you? You must have a lot to see to.

I smiled politely and tried to take Elmer's hand, but it was no longer there. I looked around in confusion. He'd sat down again and was busy rolling his goodie bag shut.

The worst part about the first Christmas as a widow wasn't that Lasse wasn't there. It was writing the tags for the presents. Two sad little poems.

To Elmer from Mum.
To Kaj from Mum.

New Year's Eve. Champagne, lobster soup, roast beef and marzipan ring cake. I wore stilettos in my own apartment and streamers around my neck, stood by the window and watched my dad, my little brother and Elmer lighting fireworks in the street.

The smell of gunpowder that wafted in when my mum and I opened the window and shouted *goddamn it, Asbjørn* in unison, as he ran down Borggade with a lit Roman candle raised above his head, my dad and Elmer cheering him on.

And the fizzing balls of fire shooting up and winking out before they lost momentum, and at midnight the sky over Aarhus erupting into psychedelic palm trees and crackling glitter, and me blubbering away, shedding tears of everything.

VII

When life as a single mum kicked in for real in the new year, Lasse's absence became a problem of a more practical nature. Emma worked at a nursery during the day, and in the evenings we pulled through together, but at night I was on my own. I was the only one who could comfort the boys when they cried.

I never got more than two hours' sleep at a time before one of them needed me. Either Kaj would need feeding or Elmer was thirsty; one of them would slurp away while the other shat the bed through their pyjamas and the sheets, or else there were earaches and nightmares. When Kaj finally surrendered to sleep, Elmer would wake up far too early, and on it went, around and around in circles.

The sound of a child whimpering in the night didn't trigger my maternal instincts, only my nausea.

They weren't picked up out of bed by a pair of patient and loving arms. I just wanted them asleep.

I gave them dummies, breasts, cups of water, and shushed them into eternity, my feet freezing and the wrinkles in my forehead deepening as I sat with my head resting on the frame of Elmer's cot, mumbling my way through desperate goodnight songs as Kaj screamed from the other room.

For hours every evening I held Kaj in my arms and tried to rock him to sleep, but as soon as I lay him down, my back aching, tucked him into the depths of his cot and withdrew my arms, his eyes would fly open and he would wail even louder than before, and I'd have to start all over again.

Waa! Waa! Waa! he went as I rocked him, as I walked around in the dark, shaking my head and whispering to myself:

This is pure torture. How the fuck am I supposed to be able to function tomorrow? What the fuck am I supposed to do?

I wedged the dummy in his mouth, the plastic collided with his gums and he spat it out. I put it between my own teeth, rocked him faster, deeper, closed my eyes and threw my head back, thinking: An ape would have long since thrown this screaming baby from a treetop to be crushed on the jagged rocks below.

His crying reached a crescendo and I gaped down at him in disbelief.

If you don't stop, Mum will put you down and you'll have to scream yourself to sleep, I said.

Except I didn't.

I squatted and stood up quickly, squatted again, but it didn't make a difference, and for a moment I could easily imagine – not understand exactly, but imagine – what it was that drove some people to shake their children to the point of brain damage. I stood up quickly again, I chewed the dummy, he screamed, then I tightened my hold on his little body and squeezed, hard. I didn't know I was going to do it until I'd done it and he'd let out a choked little squeak. Horrified, I relaxed my grip and started crying along with him, my tears darkening the faded baby duvet cover.

When he'd finally calmed down, I perched on the edge of

the bed, still holding him in my arms. I didn't have the heart to let go.

I took in his beautiful eyelids, the little silver pools in the corner of each eye, his chubby hands and the dimples on his fingers, the fingers that even in sleep gripped one side of my shirt tight, and I whispered:

Little monkey boy, your hands think they're grabbing hold of breast fur, silly thing, I hope you never get bigger and smarter. You just need your mum, that's me, I'm all you've got, and I need you even more than you need me, because if I don't have you, I'm nothing.

And I thought: A child is the hook a parent hangs their life on.

But what a life. Out of sheer desperation I'd started keeping a record on a pad of paper on the bedside table. I wrote down the time when one of the children woke up and the time when they fell asleep again. Documentation of the horrendous nights, or proof: this was really happening. It wasn't just me, exaggerating.

OK, I might have exaggerated a little, I'd have to admit in the morning; but there it was, in black and white, for anyone who cared to look.

On good nights, when I managed to get both children to sleep at the same time, I'd struggle to fall asleep myself, the ghost of Lasse hanging over me, the next day's meals and appointments to be planned.

I lay there, silently screaming to myself. *Sleep! Sleep for fuck's sake, now's your chance.* But the more I repeated the words, the less they worked.

Those were the nights I ended up directing my anger at Lasse.

I threw myself on to my back, beat the duvet to one side and raised both my middle fingers up at the sky, spitting out into the dark:

Fuck you, you fucking idiot, fuck you and your piece-of-shit star! You pushed yourself too far and left me alone with all of this, sitting up there all dead and not lifting a finger and still they're calling you a fucking saint. It's your fucking fault I can't enjoy Elmer and Kaj's childhoods, fuck you for giving me a piece-of-shit baby who screams and screams and screams. I hate you, Lasse!

I dreamed I'd kept some of Lasse's sperm alive in my uterus. After Kaj was born, they'd sneaked up one of my fallopian tubes and fertilized one of my eggs. Now I'd have to give birth to yet another of Lasse's children. Another chance to love him and honour his memory.

God save Lasse. Halle-fucking-lujah.

The sight of Emma, evening after evening, taking over, taking Kaj and his duvet from me and rocking him in her arms. The feeling of panic, watching them. Waves of tiredness rolling over me, crashing. Seasick.

My friends suggested I put Kaj on the bottle so he'd be less dependent on me and they'd be more able to help.

An insane suggestion.

Breastfeeding was one of the few things that made me feel like a good mother. It was something I could do. When I ran out of ways to calm Kaj down, my breasts were my secret weapon. And what if he ended up liking the bottle? I'd already lost so much of myself, as a person, a woman, a mother. I wouldn't let this tragedy claim any more victims. My breast milk was the glue just about holding me together.

They asked whether I'd tried putting Kaj in the pushchair and leaving him on the balcony. The fresh air would give him a good night's sleep, they assured me.

I hadn't. I bundled him up in a woollen suit, hat and thermal socks. I pulled another pair of socks over his clenched hands, as he screamed and screamed. I put the dummy in his mouth, laid him in the carrycot and wedged a duvet around him and a blanket around the duvet, then I put the dummy back in his mouth and carried the carrycot out to the balcony, pulled the rain cover off the pushchair, pushed the pushchair's awning back, slid the carrycot into the pushchair, put the dummy back in his mouth, got flicked by the zip of the rain cover in a gust of wind, wrestled it under control, pulled the awning back over him, opened the awning again to get to the baby monitor I'd laid at the foot of the carrycot, turned the baby monitor on, pulled the awning back over him, put the dummy back in his mouth, settled the rain cover over the pushchair and began to rock it back and forth like a boat in the sea in a storm.

At first he screamed, then whimpered. Then he stopped crying entirely and I could hear him sucking calmly, a cute little sound.

Then he slept.

It worked.

Sleep.

I waited.

I tiptoed back into the bedroom and closed the balcony door behind me. Put my ear to the baby monitor, could hardly believe my luck. He was sleeping.

I pulled off my jumper and trousers and released the pinch of my nursing bra underneath my shirt, shimmied one strap down my shoulder and pulled the bra out of the opposite armhole, then lay down in the middle of the bed.

Ååååhhh! All that space, all mine.

I rolled on to my side and could already feel the saliva dribbling out of my mouth and into a slimy circle on the pillow.

Sweet Jesus, I'd made it, this was the night I would sleep.

And I did. Sleep overwhelmed me almost instantly and I fell blithely into its arms.

Waa! went the baby monitor, two minutes later.

No! I cried back, to no avail.

WAA! Kaj screamed, and I struggled up, wrapped the duvet around me and went back out on to the balcony in my socks, put the dummy back in his mouth, which screamed and screamed as I rocked the pushchair back and forth, back and forth, the wind whipping around us, my hair blowing into my mouth, and his crying sending signals to my breasts: *lactate*. And their treacherous leaking milk, which hardened like ice on the inside of my top. And the knowledge that even if I miraculously managed to get him to sleep again, by that time I'd be so mad, so cold and wet, that I'd have close to no chance of falling asleep myself.

Which is when I happened to look across the backyard and see, through the window of another apartment, a woman lying naked on her back on a dining table, an equally naked man between her legs. He thrust into her shudderingly, climatically, I couldn't not see it. There it was: what I no longer had access to. And here I was: what I'd been reduced to.

To wake to crying, always.

Shuffling along to nursery one morning with the kids in the double pushchair and lost in my own incoherent stream of thought, I turned to cross the road –

A car braked so hard that for a split second it nearly lurched up on to its front wheels. Elmer turned his wool-clad head to face it, almost close enough to see right through the grille into the engine.

I was still on the pavement, in relative safety, my eyes darting from Elmer to the driver and back to Elmer again, and only then did I notice the panic reverberating through my shoulders.

Terrified, I dragged the pushchair back up on to the kerb as the driver yelled from inside his car. I caught his eye. He was gesticulating wildly with his arms, his mouth forming the words: *WHAT ARE YOU DOING?*

Sorry! I shouted. I don't know! I don't know what the fuck I'm doing!

What was I doing?

I couldn't work out why I was so determined to keep this up, why I was seemingly incapable of asking for more help. Before the birth it had made sense for me to do it all myself, I hadn't wanted to shuttle Elmer from adult to adult, but did it still make sense? Was my judgement flawed?

I couldn't shake the thought.

When I looked in the mirror, I began to suspect the woman staring back at me was a crazy person. The tar-black mascara, perfectly combed through every eyelash, gave me a sinister look, especially considering the circumstances in which I usually applied it: before we left the apartment in the mornings, both children crying at my feet.

Surely I was the problem, the reason the kids were so unmanageable. They calmed down when we visited my parents. But when we visited my parents there was no such thing as bedtime or dinner time or tidiness. There were delightful, distracting things everywhere, children everywhere, and I was the only one checking my watch.

Thoughts chasing each other around my head.

Because what if my strength had evolved into a kind of martyrdom, what if I was holding the children hostage? And the next logical thought, a far more painful one: what if they'd be better off with somebody else?

I asked my psychologist for advice.

He said I was only human, that I ought to let people help me more. He observed that I'd seemed more listless than usual recently; he suspected it could be the early signs of depression. A completely normal reaction to such an insane load, he said.

I nodded gallantly, but as soon as I was out of his office, the tears started rolling out of me.

*

I decided to prove him wrong. A couple of days later I went to my doctor to be checked for depression. I filled out the questionnaire as superficially as possible, holding her gaze with my mascaraed eyes as I sat upright, breastfeeding Kaj, and left just shy of a diagnosis.

The next time I saw my psychologist, I set him straight.

I wasn't depressed, I was grieving and I was tired, that's what the test said, and that made all the difference. I emerged from his office, triumphant.

The test was proof: I was superhuman.

But it became increasingly impossible to keep up appearances. I experienced everything through the lens of exhaustion; there wasn't enough concealer in the world to mask the dark circles around my eyes.

My breath stank of insomnia and diarrhoea; I felt unremittingly nauseous and hungover. As if the world was always about to come crashing down. Or I was. Or we were about to crash into each other.

When I left the apartment, I moved with the utmost caution. Repeatedly patting my pockets to make sure I hadn't forgotten anything.

Keys. Phone. Purse. Keys.

The sun didn't warm my skin, it hurt my eyes. If a toy car drove into a chair leg with a loud *bang*, I shuddered.

All the while, resentment simmering within.

Nappies and breast pads, yellow shit and brown shit and black shit and red blood, left shoes and right shoes, sticky fingers in child gloves, snot trails on my shoulder, changing bags and bin bags, *no* and *Mu-um* and *waa*, cracker crumbs in my cleavage, let-down reflex in my nipples, sweat under an itchy hat, duvets clumping up at the bottom of sour-smelling covers.

But people still called me strong, and when they did I stood up a little straighter: yes, I was. I was.

Deep down I missed myself. The self I'd been, back when I was neither strong nor alone. I missed the lovestruck woman cruising Route 1 through California with her boyfriend, the lively mother in our photos from Prague, the journalism student with ambitions that stretched above and beyond motherhood.

And I missed the time right after Lasse's death too, the way my feelings then were so close at hand and focused on him. Back when all there was was grief and love.

I'd thrown out the last half a bag of mouldy ravioli – the same bag Lasse's oblivious hands had fastened shut with an elastic band – and I'd moved his clothes aside to make way for baby-grows and muslins in the wardrobe.

He was gone and I knew it.

But still I doubted I'd ever be genuinely happy again, still I spent most of my time wishing life would go to hell. The life left to me to live, the life Lasse no longer had access to. I apologised to him and my two fluffy-haired chicks in their stripy pyjamas, a clump of sleep in my eyes.

I'm sorry I'm not able to give you a happy childhood. I'm sorry I don't have the strength to play with you. I'm sorry for shouting. I'm sorry for being so selfish. I'm sorry I don't mention Dad any more. I'm sorry I brought you into this painful and brutal world.

And yet, occasionally, a glimpse of it.

Gratitude.

When I lay next to Kaj, and his hand closed around my little finger, so alive. I knew what it was like to hold a hand that didn't return my squeeze, and I thanked Lasse and whoever else might be listening for the very existence of this moment.

In those small, strong muscles, the entire world seemed to open up.

VIII

The days played a sluggish tag with one another. They dragged their feet over the damp asphalt and Monday laid a heavy paw on Tuesday's back and said, you're it, and Tuesday blinked in surprise and turned to look at Monday, who just shrugged, and off Tuesday traipsed in search of Wednesday, who was slumped over a sandpit, lost in thought.

And so it continued.

I ought to treat myself, everyone said.

My dad offered to look after the kids for a couple of hours so I could have some *me time*. Several people had suggested a massage, so I'd booked an appointment at an organic wellness clinic a few hundred metres from the apartment.

With the boys in the double pushchair, my dad set off on a walk. I watched them go, my arms left strangely empty.

The treatment room was warm with the smell of roses and citrus oil; drowsy harp music wafted out of discreetly placed speakers, seemingly without end. Towels were rolled up into snug sausages and piled on top of each other on a bamboo table; a lowered blind softened the light.

Feel free to put your clothes there, said the masseuse in an airy voice, waving at a stool.

Red rose petals had been scattered over the massage table, which she now removed one by one as I undressed.

I sighed in a way I hoped sounded relaxed, to signal that I'd taken my clothes off, and when she turned to face me I tried to act as if it was no big deal to be down to my knickers in broad daylight. Wondering whether she noticed my doughy belly, my cellulite-riddled butt cheeks and uneven breasts. I'd only breast-fed Kaj on one side and that breast hung slack and tired next to the other one, full to burst.

She asked me to lie down on my stomach with my face in the hole.

I crawled up on to the table and did as she'd instructed. She laid a warm towel over my legs and folded it down along with my underwear so I could feel my arse crack peeking out. Then she poured warm oil over my back. When her hands began to move up and down in long, firm strokes, I struggled to keep my breath even. It occurred to me that I hadn't been touched like this by another person in many, many months. I wanted it to stop.

It was always about Lasse, even when it wasn't.

My tears rolled down through the face hole and the masseuse's shoes rubbed out the drops as she moved around to do my neck.

When it was finally over, I averted my eyes and hastily threw my clothes back on. My breast was swollen and crying out for its baby, and I fled from the harps and lemons and ran all the way home.

I lay on the living-room floor with both kids giggling and crawling over me, making my hair static. The afternoon sun baked us in a soft orange glow and I pinched them gently on their necks, inhaled their sweet smell and felt a rare warmth coursing through me.

The feeling turned to ice.

They could die. They could die and I could die. Life was no longer a sure thing, it was cut-throat. I grabbed hold of them and squeezed their little bodies close, we had so much to lose, but they just squealed in delight, kicking to break free. It was all a game to them.

Emma left for Africa three months after Kaj was born, and the boys and I were alone again. Around the same time, my downstairs neighbour got a new lover. I'd never heard a peep from him before, but now I discovered that his bedroom was directly under our living room, and that he was gay.

It had been nearly half a year since I'd heard a man having sex. I turned down the TV volume and sat quiet as a mouse, listening to the two men below me.

One high-pitched and quick, the other deep and dominating.

I missed sex. And while my head remained convinced that sex was a Lasse thing, my body wasn't so picky.

I started fantasizing about how my friends might be in bed. Chest hair sticking out of the top of their shirts, their broad necks, and the thought of what their fingers would feel like as they met the sensitive skin on the inside of my arms.

In an elevator in Magasin with a man I'd never met and the pushchair between us, my mind darted straight over to him and crept in under his clothes, and the more I tried to pull it back, the more it insisted, clinging to his leather belt, his Adam's apple, his bottom lip. What I wouldn't do for a pair of male hands.

I longed to abandon myself to pleasure.

And it occurred to me that I could, that it wouldn't even be cheating. But I shied away from the thought. I was still a married woman; my husband was just dead.

Predictably it was now, just as things were beginning to calm down a bit, that my body decided it had needs and demanded that those needs be met. Lasse had died six months ago, and yet here I was, breaking one of the last things that had been ours.

It would be far easier to remain alone forever. A beautiful surrender. Proud and untouchable in Lasse's shadow. Mother, widow.

In February I celebrated our anniversary alone. Our love was still worth celebrating, I told myself. The memories of our wedding filled me with a staggering pain – all my memories of Lasse did – but this time I was afraid it might actually break me in two.

We got married in a snowstorm.

He stood at the altar, freshly trimmed and trim in a sleek black suit, leaning to one side so he could take in as much of me as possible as I slowly made my way down the aisle of Aarhus Cathedral.

Orchids in my hair.

My arm shook in my dad's, and he put his mouth to my ear and whispered:

One step at a time. Don't worry, try to enjoy it.

I would rather have sprinted through the church in my gold stilettos and leaped into Lasse's arms.

Later, the guests told us that Lasse had forgotten to remove the yellow stickers from the soles of his new shoes. Everyone had seen how much they'd cost when we knelt solemnly before the priest. We laughed it off, it didn't matter. We were husband and wife now, high on our own supply.

Outside, the snow fell in soft, zigzagging wads of cotton.

We were grinning so much we could barely keep our lips together for the photos. He was twenty-four, I was twenty-three, and we had no idea what throwing a party for eighty-five people entailed. We'd bought one bag of coffee and my dad had to run to Fakta for more.

I kicked my stilettos under the gift table before the starter even arrived. My toes were throbbing in pain, and before we walked out of the party and into the icy night I tied a couple of freezer bags over my feet.

Lasse picked me up, wouldn't have me walking through the snow in a wedding dress and plastic-bag slippers. We kept falling over and giggling at the spectacle we must have made for the people we passed on the streets.

On our anniversary I went to the florist and bought a pot of calla lilies for me and a bouquet of the same for him.

In the cemetery, I knelt in front of his headstone and brushed a couple of dead leaves aside before removing my gloves and resting my fingers on the hard earth I'd lowered his urn into mere months before. Winter nipped at my cheeks; the frost shuddered up through my fingertips at regular intervals.

We ought to be at a restaurant drinking wine together, I thought. I ought to be giving him a new shirt, not flowers.

Kaj was asleep in the pushchair next to his parents. It was time I got him home and warm.

Lasse wasn't an especially good cook, but he had his signature dishes. Tuna mousse, chocolate mousse, chilli con carne.

I'd never touch them – they were his. But we had a tub of chilli con carne left over in the freezer that I'd been saving especially for the occasion. It would be as if he'd made me dinner on our anniversary.

The tub was frozen fast and let out a crack when I pulled it off the bottom of the plastic drawer. I lifted the lid and inspected the hard clump with kidney beans and sweetcorn on top, coated in a thick layer of ice crystals.

We'd moved into the apartment on Borggade over a year ago. Lasse's chilli con carne was probably nearly as old. I couldn't afford a stomach bug for the sake of romance, I had kids to look after the next day.

We ate rye-bread sandwiches that evening. The lilies withered soon after.

To trade in love for strength.

I slid the wardrobe door open and reached resolutely for the dust cover that held my wedding dress. Helle stood waiting in the hall. She made a face when she saw the dress.

It was the most beautiful day, she said. What a wonderful wedding, I'll never forget . . .

She bowed her head, the corners of her mouth already drooping.

It was, it really was a wonderful day, I agreed, retreating into the kitchen for a paper bag, raising my voice so she could still hear me as I folded the dress into it. And I can't wait to see the results. Are you sure there's enough fabric for the gown as well as a shirt for Elmer?

I handed her the bag and she stood up straight and nodded.

On the day of the christening, a friend took a photo of me holding both children, all decked out in their embroidered white satin and frills. My hair is thin and my chin is double with the effort, but I'm grinning right into the camera and it's the first picture of me since Lasse where you can see the light dancing in my eyes.

Winter was exceptionally tough. The chill ate through my clothes and hammered its way into my bones. The earth froze then unfroze, only to freeze all over again.

On the 1st of April there was still snow in my parents' garden, but the sun shone in a cloudless sky and I unfolded a garden chair, unzipped my coat and sat down with my eyes closed, pulling the still-frosty air deep into my lungs as the rays warmed my face and chest.

I felt something on my knee and opened my eyes.

A bee.

We sat together, sunning ourselves for a while, then it flew off over the snow and disappeared around the corner of the house.

I was in Kvickly one afternoon with the kids in the double push-chair beside me. Elmer was eating a sandwich, Kaj was shaking a toy with bells on it, and I was peering into a fridge, trying to choose between cold cuts – they were on offer, three for two – when, all of a sudden, a man a few metres away bent a woman backwards over a freezer. She closed her eyes in delight and he kissed her passionately, his hands squeezing her buttocks as he brushed his lips over her cheek and whispered into her ear. She listened to him with her mouth wide open, then burst into irresistible laughter.

They only had eyes for each other, and I only had eyes for them.

I wanted my buttocks squeezed, my ear whispered into. I didn't want the careful caresses of well-meaning friends. I wanted to be wanted.

To my surprise I found for the first time that I was able to have this thought without shame. I let the feeling explore my body over the following days, and it met no resistance. It had nothing to do with Lasse.

For months, Lasse's elephant poster in the kids' room had been falling apart, and I'd been dutifully repairing it, taping the pieces back together. Eventually I gave up and took it down. I spread it over the floor and folded it neatly, then put it in the bin under the kitchen sink.

We couldn't keep this up.

Every day I passed the three name stickers on our postbox: Lasse, Puk and Elmer. I couldn't bear to rip his sticker off and it seemed absurd to cover it up with Kaj's name.

It was no better inside the apartment. Lasse had decorated our home. If I were to start moving things around, it would be an insult to him. His student architecture models collected dust on the walls; the old sketchbooks he'd refused to throw away filled several shelves. The cupboards were stuffed with his trousers, coats and holey socks.

He was a hoarder, and if he hadn't been so touchy about his things, I would have had an easier time getting rid of them. But I knew him, I knew he'd be perched on the edge of his star shouting *stop* every time I lugged one of the boxes down to the bins.

I longed to call the shots in my own life, to do something radical, start all over. If we stayed in the apartment on Borggade, I'd be forever trapped in Lasse's memory, binge-watching TV and listening to other people have sex through the floorboards.

So I left. I went to the bank and asked how much I could borrow as a single mum on student grants also in possession of a sizeable sum of life insurance. It was enough. They helped me calculate a realistic mortgage – one I could keep up with as long as I found a part-time job in the next year – and I began looking straight away.

I fell in love with a little yellow townhouse in a village-like corner of Aarhus. Ivy on the walls, pushchairs grazing in the back garden, laundry in baby and adult sizes hanging on the line, and people who waved from their kitchen windows.

My friends Helene and Kristine came by the week before the move to help me pack up Lasse's clothes. He still had his own rack, his shoes in neat rows.

Once we'd put the kids to sleep, we sat on my bed and gathered all his clothes in a pile between us. I pressed my face into them, but they no longer smelled of him. Now they held only my memories. I asked Kristine and Helene to fold the clothes but not to comment on them. Lasse had been their friend too.

We folded in silence. The only interruptions were wet sniffles and the scratchy sound as our hands brushed the flaps of the cardboard boxes.

Helene folded up the Pearl Jam concert. Kristine laid the arms of the new father neatly over his back and folded him in half with his chest on top. I straightened the bridegroom's boxer shorts and rolled them into a sausage. Once we'd made our way through the pile, we closed the boxes and sealed them with gaffer tape.

Just short of a year after Lasse's death, I sat in my own living room surrounded by boxes and people, a pile of takeaway pizzas stacked on the coffee table.

We were spent and emotional after hours of lifting and carrying and lifting again. My parents had taken care of the kids for the day, while my friends carted furniture into various rooms, bickering over who was strong enough to lift the heavy end of the sofa, attempting to assemble baby beds without the instructions. After Elmer and Kaj were asleep in their new room, we sat in the glow of a floor lamp and we were adults together, we were young together; we drank beer and my mum told an inappropriate anecdote about sex with my dad, and everyone spluttered with laughter, and I tried to be annoyed but couldn't because I was laughing too, because of the foamy beer and the feeling bubbling up inside: of something not quite yet in sight but now at least within reach.

We landed in a kind of everyday, a little life. Full of routines and meaning, the number of good days on the rise.

The boys played in the bath in the evenings and I sat with them, reading a book with rolled-up trousers and my feet submerged in the warm water. We watched TV, we lit candles on overcast mornings, we argued, they fought, I washed up, Kaj learned to walk and chase spiders, I laid out clothes for the next day in three little piles, Elmer started drawing, I wrote a poem about getting on a bus and falling in love, we turned the music up and danced after dinner again. I baked buns at weekends. Sometimes we waved goodnight to Dad on the star, but most of the time we didn't.

Lasse faded.

I could no longer recall his face every time I shut my eyes. I had to conjure up a particular detail first – his Adam's apple, his wonky front tooth – in order to put the rest of the puzzle pieces together and make him whole again.

And yet he still managed to find a way to appear, in all his clarity, just when I hadn't called for him.

When Elmer pursed his lips in concentration, there he was.

When I warmed Kaj's feet in my hands, it was like holding tiny versions of Lasse's, with their funny high arches and toes scrunched up like they were cracking a nut.

But the Lasse who lived inside me was finally coming to rest. The first time I thought about him without grief or anger, I felt as light as a feather.

I had you, that was real, I said into the room, and nobody heard it.

For his third birthday, Elmer got an orange bike with stabilizers. I'd hidden it under a blanket in the middle of the living room; it looked like a little animal with frayed edges. Elmer squatted down and lifted the blanket a few centimetres, then turned to face me, his eyes shining.

The trees had already cast the year off and on to the pavement around us, the sun was high in the crystal blue sky, and Elmer sat on his new bike, looking anxiously from his hands on the handlebars to his feet on the pedals, held upright by the stabilizers.

He hesitated, then pushed one of the pedals with his foot and the bike jerked a little way forward, making him jump.

And again, Elmer, I said. There's nothing to be afraid of, I'm right here.

He shifted his weight on to the other foot and the bike jerked again, sending little pebbles scuttling away as they met with the rubber wheel. He looked fearfully up at me.

It's OK, you just need to get going. I'll help you.

I put a hand between his shoulder blades and gave him a gentle nudge. He held on to the handlebars for dear life as the bike began to roll forward.

With one hand on his back and the other on Kaj's pushchair, I walked for a while alongside him. He was heavy at first, but soon began to take over. First one leg, then the other, and, as the bike started moving faster, he lifted his gaze from the handlebars to the pavement in front of him, and I broke into a jog to keep up. Until I couldn't, and my hand left his back, and he carried on wobbling down the pavement away from us.

Kaj sat up in the pushchair and craned his neck to see.

I exhaled.

Look, Kaj. Elmer can cycle!

He was already a fair way ahead of us.

I cheered.

You're doing it by yourself now, Elmer. You're riding a bike!

Two on the sofa. Father and child asleep.

A baby duvet draped over them, the morning sunshine caught by the greasy fingerprints on the garden door. I'm standing next to them in silence.

The man's breathing is slow and heavy, the baby's light and chirruping. The baby is lying face down on top of the man, his little body rising and falling with every breath his dad takes. Sometimes the tiny legs kick under the duvet.

The man is naked apart from a pair of black boxer shorts. He's lying in an awkward position with his head on the armrest and one leg supporting himself on the floor, the other stretched out along the sofa, but somehow he still looks relaxed.

A mess of a living room: Elmer's blue school bag thrown into one corner, four plates and the dregs of a bottle of sparkling water from yesterday's dinner on the dining table. We were all too busy with the new family member to do anything about it.

The smell of tomato sauce.

On the windowsill, our family photos: Elmer and Kaj reluctantly holding hands for the photographer; our wedding; Lasse running his first half-marathon, waving to us.

My breasts have swollen with milk overnight; the parquet

floor feels warm under my bare feet. Standing here, I can't help but shake my head at us. What were we thinking, having a baby? I close my eyes as the tears come rushing up. We have far too much to lose.

It's 6 a.m. and soon the baby's brothers will wake in their bunks and come clattering down the stairs looking for us, demanding to know why we weren't upstairs in bed. We're here, I'll say.

We're here.

ACKNOWLEDGEMENTS

I'm eternally grateful to everyone who was there for me and the children.

A special thanks to: my huge family, Lasse's family, Helene Storgaard Christiansen, Kristine Gottlieb Knudsen, Olm Jakobsen, Kira Bang-Olsson, Tinush Helles Hansen, Camilla Huus Kamstrup, Marianne Riiskjær Gravgaard, Kenneth Sletten Christensen, Karianne Halse, Espen Lunde Nielsen, Sophie Rye Hansen, Allan Bech Hansen, Pernille Juul, Jimmi Hassel Nielsen, Poul Henning Bartholin, Linda Vilhelmsen, Katharine Simpson, Jo Carlsen, the staff at Storkereden Nursery and Godsbanen in Aarhus.

Thank you to my Danish editor, Charlotte Jørgensen, for our close collaboration on this book, thanks to my agent, Laurence Laluyaux, and to my UK editor, Hermione Thompson, for the support, insight and guidance.

And to Hazel Evans, my wonderful English translator: you have gone above and beyond for this novel. I am deeply grateful to you.

Most of all, thank you, Pier. *Solo con te.*